The Bridge at Fall's End

A Nun's Drift story

Sheila Jacobs

malcolm down

PUBLISHING

First published 2026 by Malcolm Down Publishing Ltd
www.malcolmdown.co.uk

28 27 26 25 24   7 6 5 4 3 2 1

British Library Cataloguing in Publication Data
A catalogue record for this book is available from the British Library.

ISBN 978-1-917455-53-4

Cover design by Esther Kotecha
Art direction by Sarah Grace

Printed in the UK

Bridge illustration by Shutterstock
Rocks illustration by Freepik

Dedication

Soli Deo Gloria

Thanks

To Malcolm Down
and Helen Hudson

Further thanks to

Ellie Ake, Matt Harding, Jenny Golding, Maria Redmond, Alison Gray, Mandy Merritt, Tina Allen, Danni Belgrove, Phil Steward, and my lovely Spiritual Companionship group

For my dad, Keith Jacobs

And everyone who liked *Nun's Drift*
Or who like me.

Contents

Introduction

The next episode in the story of the residents of *Nun's Drift* features an enigmatic bridge that seemingly leads to nowhere. While I've used this as a 'word picture' to illustrate themes in the book, it was inspired by a place I discovered when I was cycling with a friend during the summer of 2024.

This book is a further weaving together of Meg, Barny, Rosemary and Jason's inner worlds. The challenges of letting go of what we cannot control, of our proclivity to judge what we don't know or understand, and the importance of accepting ourselves, our choices and our lives, while trusting in a God who extends grace, will hopefully mean that you find something helpful and thought-provoking within the pages.

In the end, it's all about focusing on the Good Shepherd who loves us, who has a plan for us, and trusting him – even when life doesn't always make sense.

The 'action' takes place during the Easter season.

I hope you enjoy it.

Sheila Jacobs
Halstead, Spring 2026

PART ONE

Meg's Story

Letting Go

You know, I promised myself it would never happen again. But it has.

Even trying to keep something 'light', just 'friendship' doesn't work.

At least, not for me.

Sighing, I raise my eyes and take in the scene.

There's not much in Fall's End, really. You come along the winding lane from Nun's Drift with a sense of expectancy, only to pass under a railway bridge, spotting a rather shabby-looking garage with a few second-hand cars for sale just beyond. St Mary's is on the left; a Suffolk wool church, too big for such a small village, set back from the road on higher ground, approached by many well-worn steps; it's stately and out of place, a relic of more prosperous times.

There's a sharp turn, and on the right there's what they call the 'market square' – some whitewashed timber buildings, looking as if they're falling forward, they're so old – a hardware shop, a baker's, a 'convenience store', a pharmacy and a charity shop facing a couple of benches on the gently sloping grass verge, and what amounts to a 'square' with a few parking spaces. Following the road on straight, you come across the kind of new estate they're building everywhere, and beyond that, fields, then a couple of quaint hamlets; but if you take a left turn by the King's Arms, passing the old windmill (open to visitors every Saturday in the summer), you eventually arrive in Smith's Common – very upmarket, looking down its rather lofty nose at the residents of Fall's End.

I come here on Thursdays; there are market stalls in the square, and some of the produce is good quality. The guy who sells cheese is good-looking, and likes a chat. Today, though, I find I'm not much in the mood for banter.

I admit, I've been careless with people's emotions in the past and that's caused problems. Of course, now I've started to think about the more *spiritual* aspect of my life, I'm constantly being challenged on the way I think and live. I know for sure I don't want *feelings.* Too serious, too scary. Maybe that's why I always seem to chase the unattainable.

I'm sitting on a bench, thinking. Late March clouds are scudding across a cool blue sky, and there are a few spring flowers in wooden tubs outside the shops. The residents are clearly trying to cheer the place up, but it can never compete with Nun's Drift, the idyllic village where I live. I stare at the tubs, but the multicoloured primula aren't really registering.

I've got a friend. He's cute, he's exciting, but I never thought he'd fall for me. And then there's this other guy in my life. I really like him, but yes, he's unavailable.

My friend Rosemary comes out of the charity shop, flustered. She'd been donating some old china, and her husband, Arthur, has the car today, so I'd offered to give her a lift. The café – *my* café – is under the care of my aunt, Lou. But we need to get back. I can't let Lou bear the burden too long on her own, even though it's my half day off. She's not up to it, poor soul. She was going to get married in February but they had to postpone the wedding. The fella she's (allegedly still) marrying has 'issues'. He'll need a fair bit of help before he commits to marriage. Anyway, that's what they're saying.

Rosemary bustles over, and she seems out of breath.

'It's no use!' She settles herself beside me, pulling a packet of wet wipes out of the enormous bag she carries. She's got just about everything in there. 'I just don't like her.'

'Who?' I shield my eyes from the sun's strengthening rays.

She wipes her face. 'That Bellwood girl! She's working in the charity shop. She's their new manager. She used to work in the library in Fairleigh. *You* know . . . Paula! Tall, thin, serious, miserable. Lives with her mother. And *she's* not a barrel of laughs, either.'

Oh yeah . . . the old woman who runs the antiques shop in Nun's Drift.

'Sorry, Rosemary, I'm not quite with it today.'

Rosemary shakes her head and I admire, as always, the way her hairdresser gets those blonde highlights just right. She's not bad-looking for an oldie, although she needs to shift a bit of weight. She mutters something about needing to keep fit. Then she grabs a chocolate bar from her bag and offers me some before wolfing down a fair-sized chunk. Her phone rings and as she drags it out of her bag, my eyes rest on her fuchsia nails. I casually glimpse the screen.

Rev Jason Dazely.

'Oh, hello, Vicar,' she's saying. 'Yes! I wanted to talk to you . . . yes, the list . . . the most wonderful plan for an amazing social project! Well . . . alright, that might be a slight exaggeration . . . I want to help a few people . . . You've looked at it? Well, I was going to change – oh. Well, later will be fine. Five thirty? Right.' She ends the call and blows out her cheeks. 'How on earth am I going to tell him I don't even *like* the people I ought to help?'

'Rosemary, you're one of the most honest people I know!' I laugh. 'I take it Paula Bellwood's on your list, then?'

She sighs. 'Come on, let's get some of that delicious applewood cheddar. The man who sells the cheese is nice-looking, isn't he?'

'You've been hanging around with Daisy Parker too much! Married three times – so far – drives a red sports car and says, "I'm older, darling, I'm not dead."'

My affected voice is very Daisy, and Rosemary laughs with me. 'Bless her. Oh, the phone again – no, it's yours. Meg! Your phone.'

I get it out of my pocket. *Barny.* I don't answer it. Rosemary narrows her eyes but doesn't ask me any questions.

'You know,' she says later, as we walk to the car with our packets of cheese, 'I've always thought of Fall's End as Nun's Drift's poorer, less attractive cousin. But there's one time of the year the village comes into its own – the wonderful Passion Play at Easter. Only a few weeks away!'

Yes, late this year, end of April. Rosemary witters on for a bit about this 'amazing' play, which sounds to me like more of a tedious trudge from one village to the next than anything that will set the world alight.

We're on the way home, and she's still talking. 'Poor old Fall's End. Usually such a boring place. Although I suppose there's the bridge ... *That's* a bit different.'

I glance at her. How is the bridge by that old garage in any way 'a bit different' to every other railway bridge in England?

'Don't look at me as if I'm losing the plot!' She's seen my quizzical look. 'The bridge at Fall's End! Well, it's in-between Nun's Drift and Fall's End, really.'

OK, different bridge! I crash the gears, cursing under my breath, but she hasn't heard me.

She starts to explain. She says this bridge crosses a lake where it narrows, and it used to lead to a fine mansion, once used by friars. But the house was demolished years ago and now it's a stone bridge to nowhere. Her voice turns wistful. 'I used to play there, as a child. Wasn't meant to, the adults said it was a creepy place, dangerous water, all that ... but we all thought it was such fun, building dens, climbing trees!'

She's staring out of the window as we arrive in Nun's Drift, primroses clothing the grassy banks in cheery welcome, pink blossom on cherry trees in several gardens, while daffodils nod their glorious golden heads on the green.

We pull up outside the café.

'Look, Meg, will you come with me to see the vicar? I could do with your input.'

'Er . . . sorry, work.'

'The café shuts at five,' she replies, smartly.

'I'm – look, I'm a bit busy . . .'

'No, you're not.' She's trying to yank open the creaky old door of the creaky old Land Rover. 'I happen to know your *friend*, that Barny Baines person, is away at the moment, visiting his father.' She's manoeuvring her plump body out of the car. 'Honestly! When your aunt pulls herself together, she can buy a new vehicle.'

'I'm thinking of buying a car!' She slams the door. 'A red Peugeot . . . in Fall's End garage,' I mumble. But no one hears.

The vicar looks as uncomfortable as I feel, as I walk into that room. His study is being redecorated after some sort of incident involving his cat and we are consequently meeting in the sitting room.

He's ensconced in his worn-out sofa, moved from his study and shoved into the already overcrowded room. None of his furniture matches; it all looks as if it's seen better days. He makes an effort to stand as we arrive, but Rosemary says, 'Oh, please don't get up, Vicar!' so he does a weird bounce back into his squashy seat.

There are two wingback chairs, one facing him across the dated, glass-topped coffee table, and one to the side. I slip into the second one, just beating Rosemary to it. She frowns at me and parks herself opposite him.

The sitting room is high-ceilinged and overlooks his front garden, the sweeping driveway and the white blossom hedgerow that I think might be blackthorn. Or is it hawthorn? I make a mental note to ask Rosemary, later. She knows all about horticultural things, Arthur being involved in the local gardening club. The blue skies of earlier have clouded over, and dots of rain are falling. I stare out of the window. The vicar's car seems very white in the greyness.

'Thanks for coming,' he says. 'Er . . . both of you.'

I nod in his general direction. Just enough of a glimpse to notice the dark, floppy fringe, the outline of a fairly well-built guy a few years older than me. I don't allow myself to look into the brown eyes.

'Flora's gone home. I need to make you some tea, don't I?' Jason says, a little helplessly.

'I'll make it, Vicar,' responds Rosemary. 'I know how useless you – I mean, I'm sure I can find the teabags.'

'No, I'll do it.' I get up quickly. I don't want to be left alone with him.

I hear the low murmur of chat while I stand waiting for the kettle to boil in the large kitchen, which really does need an upgrade. The walls are cream and cracked, and the elderly kitchen units are painted in a pale lemon stained by too many carelessly tossed teabags. I love the pine dresser, though, and the pine table and chairs, too; they seem real, not the fake kind. I lean back against the solid table and sigh. The murmur from the sitting room ebbs and flows like the tide; it goes quiet, and all I can hear is the loud ticking of the grandfather clock in the hallway. I jump as the phone rings. Barny again. I ignore it. Raindrops slide down the square-paned window like tears. I bite my lip.

The Reverend Jason Dazely. Attractive, kind, great sense of humour, single.

And he's taken a vow of celibacy.

The kettle boils, I pour the tea and find a tray, which has a poppy motif on it. Placing the mugs on the tray, I notice that several of them are also decorated with poppies. *Perhaps Jason is keen on remembering things*, I think, ironically. Like the touch of a hand, a look too long held, and embarrassment.

'Here you go.' I slap the tray down with a clatter on the coffee table.

'Good gracious,' exclaims Rosemary. 'You put that down with a bang!'

'I don't know where your biscuits are . . .' I look at him now, thinking I'm being too offhand, and he catches my eye.

'Oh . . . er . . . cupboard above the microwave.' He clears his throat and looks away. 'Anyhow, Rosemary, you were saying?'

'I was wondering where you got this table, Vicar. I'm terribly sorry, but it looks like something you might have got out of a skip in the 1970s.'

He laughs as I leave the room. I do like his laugh, it's so rich. 'Ah, that. Not guilty. It comes with the territory.'

I locate the biscuits, and bring the tin – covered in cute cats – into the sitting room, setting it on the table with more care than I did the tray. Jason is leaning forward on his sofa, gazing at Rosemary as she talks. I wonder if he really does find what she's saying engaging, or whether it's part of his vicar training – looking interested when people are boring.

Rosemary is momentarily distracted as she eyes the biscuit tin, and wrenches open the lid.

'You do like your cats!' she observes, but Jason ruefully remarks that anything to do with cats – including the real one in the vicarage – was the preference of the previous incumbent. Jason hasn't been in Nun's Drift that long, I remember. *I've known him nearly a year!*

'Well, Vicar,' Rosemary says through a mouthful of custard cream, 'you've read the list. It just came to me in the night.'

'So you said.' Jason casts his eye down the crumpled piece of paper he's holding.

'Can you see it properly?' Rosemary asks. 'It's a bit dark in here!'

I for one am glad of the badly lit room; too much unforgiving light would show up my laughter lines. *Meg, you're twenty-six. You have no lines.* Answer: *I'm twenty-seven in May. And yes, I do have lines.* But why do I care whether Jason notices them or not?

I sigh. It must have been a loud sigh because both of them suddenly look at me.

'What?' I say, defensively.

'You don't approve of Archie, Meg?'

I probably seemed confused, because Rosemary continues, briskly, 'Oh, so sorry, I thought you were making a comment! So, anyway . . . we have Archie Gainsford, the Thompson-Traceys' gamekeeper; Alec Mayfield . . . although my husband has befriended him, they go to the gardening club together – and Paula . . . um . . . Paula Bellwood . . .'

'I think we can leave Alec safely in your husband's hands,' Jason smiles. *He has such a great smile.* I study a picture on the wall. Not sure what it is, just a load of pink smudges. The wall is the same cream as the kitchen, and the curtains are brown. Not very exciting. Like Jason. *Well, he isn't, is he? Not my type at all. But then why . . .* 'I was thinking,' Jason is saying, 'we could include Ally Thompson-Tracey.'

'Ally!' Rosemary's eyes widen. 'Why? She's a difficult girl, I grant you, but I wouldn't have thought . . . well . . . she's not *needy*.'

'Isn't she?'

Well, you should know, Jason. I take a sip of my tea. *You go horse riding with her often enough.*

Rosemary's shaking her head. 'She's got the Young Farmers . . .'

I stifle a snigger and she frowns.

'I often invite her for a meal, or to my little gathering on Tuesday evenings,' she continues. 'She pops along when she isn't busy at the stables. And Meg's about the same age . . .'

'She's older than me,' I say, curtly.

Rosemary stares at me, perplexed. 'What I'm trying to say is, we're encouraging a friendship.'

Who's we? I nearly say it. *I don't like Ally. She doesn't like me. She wanted Barny and he turned her down. And now she's after Jason, and I . . .*

'Look,' says Jason, 'we'll trust your husband with Alec. But we can include Archie and Paula, definitely. We can give extra time and thought about how to reach out to them. But let's add Ally to the list, right?'

'Well . . . if you think . . .' Rosemary takes another custard cream.

'Archie lives alone with only an old dog for company. Ally hasn't got many what I'd call proper friends . . .' *Except for you, Jason.* I reach out and grab a biscuit before Rosemary eats them all. 'And Paula and her mother are . . .'

'Miserable,' Rosemary sprays biscuit. 'Oh, I do beg your pardon, Vicar.' She reaches out to wipe down his jumper but he leans back so fast I can hardly contain a laugh.

'Hmm . . . if you've got Ally coming to your group, and Meg's befriending her, that sounds fine.' He glances in my direction with a smile but manages to not actually look at me. 'Keep an eye on her, will you?' *What, like you do?* 'So, Archie and Paula, and Meg's looking after Ally.'

I want to say, 'Wouldn't you rather do it?' but don't.

'There are so many people, Vicar,' says Rosemary, plaintively. 'But we can't cover them all. Maybe other groups can target – I mean, think about – other needy souls, but these are enough for my little group. I'm busy, Meg's busy, Daisy runs a business and Flora's got her lodger to keep an eye on – that Barny character.'

That Barny character!

'Actually, Daisy said we should include him on the list, but . . .' Rosemary looks at me at this point, and I hope my warning stare is enough to keep her glossy lips shut.

'Ah, don't worry about Barny,' Jason says, reaching for the depleted biscuit tin. 'His landlady's on the case and so am I.'

I'm surprised no one adds, *And so's Meg.*

The next morning in the café, I'm putting the Belgian buns on display, thinking about Rosemary's idea to help the super-lonely, and wondering why I don't feel at all inclined to do so. Maybe it's because I often feel lonely myself. I shouldn't, really, and I wonder why I do. Of course, I'd never admit it to anyone.

I wipe my hands on my apron and think about it. I'm happy here. I've got Rosemary, Arthur, my aunt, Lou, and her partner, Tony – who she lives with now, at the farm, so I have the flat above the tearoom to myself. I love working in the café, and my aunt leaves the day-to-day running of it to me. Well, she's caught up with other things – mainly Tony, a recovering alcoholic, and his niece, who seems to have 'become wayward', as Rosemary so quaintly puts it, or 'gone rogue' as Barny says. My dad lives in High Wycombe, he's fit and well and has a better social life than I do, and I absolutely love the picturesque and friendly Nun's Drift. So I have nothing to complain about . . .

The bell tinkles and someone steps into the café.

'Hey.' A familiar, light voice.

Barny Baines! Tall, lean and fair-haired; he's attractive and he knows it. He walks to the counter in that relaxed, casual way of his.

'Oh, I didn't expect you till next week!'

'Ah, well. Just couldn't wait to get back . . .'

I'm arranging the buns, eyes fixed on them now, staying on my side of the counter.

'Is your phone permanently off or something?' he asks.

I find his question intrusive and I feel irritated.

'I'm here alone at the moment. Rosemary's coming in to cover me while . . .' I look up. 'I've got a load of herb scones to make. Can we talk later?'

'I only want a cup of coffee,' he says, rather mournfully, and I feel sorry for him.

'Yes – of course. Cappuccino?'

'Americano.' He stretches. 'Need to wake up – been a long drive. Got to go and see Old Dazzles about a job.'

I wish he wouldn't call Jason 'Old Dazzles'. Still, perhaps it's an affectionate nickname. They're friends, after all.

'How's your dad?' Nearly forgot to ask, placing the coffee in front of him.

'Not great, but he's out of hospital.' He leans across the counter. I take a step backwards. I can see from his surprised expression that he didn't expect me to move away. 'You alright?'

'I'm really busy, Barny.' My tone is too terse.

I make an excuse, got to check on something, and go into the kitchen. When I come back a few minutes later, he's gone, and his full cup of coffee is still on the counter.

The red Peugeot has been sold. But there's a blue Suzuki which has an engine the size of Arthur's lawnmower, and I can just about afford it. It's seven years old, and the driver's door has been keyed, so they're going to respray it before I can take possession of it.

I'm sitting in the Land Rover. I've left Rosemary in charge of the café for too long, but I really don't want to go back right now. Something pops into my mind. I make a decision.

I'm going to try to find that mysterious bridge at Fall's End. Not sure why; but the thought that Rosemary played there as a kid – or even trying to imagine her as younger than she is now (pushing sixty) – well, it's got me interested. Why did I always imagine her as a good child, sitting at home doing collage with beads and feathers and glitter and glue – not building dens and climbing trees? Must be the girly smart nails, smart hair, smart bungalow . . .

I make a few enquiries at the garage, then find the footpath opposite the church, and wander along a wide, tractor-pitted grass and mud track beside a field that will be swaying with yellow, bearded barley in a few months' time. Walking carefully, avoiding too much mud, I turn right, tracing the outline of a meadow with a piebald pony in it. Ahead, I suddenly see the shimmering of water behind the just-budding trees. The outline of their trunks and branches strikes me as utterly beautiful in that moment; in a few short weeks, their form will be hidden in a bright green canopy, but for now, the darkness of their structure contrasts well with the first sprinkling of foliage. In a while, the trees will all be dark and dusty, but as they hold their breath before bursting into new life, they are fresh and unique and alive. And behind, that vast lake is glistening in the morning sunshine.

Now, where's the bridge?

I follow the track; it seems to peter out in some bushes, but I battle through, and there it is in front of me.

It straddles the lake at the tapering end. I walk through half-open metalwork gates, and stand looking at a stone bridge spanning the water. I note the broken parapets, and wonder what it looked like when the bridge was new.

To the right, it's just overgrown with water weeds; but to the left, the lake is large, clear, a vast expanse of quiet and calm. It's as if time is standing still. A heron takes off from the far bank, long legs dragging behind as it soars into the silent sky.

I don't like to rest my weight on the broken parapet – so many stones are missing – but I tentatively lean over, looking down. It makes me feel slightly unbalanced, so I take a step back. It occurs to me that this is what I do; step back into safety when I feel unnerved. But what's making me feel uneasy? A random brush of the hand of a man I know has promised his God that he'll remain single forever?

He came into the café last Monday; I'm thinking of doing one of his church courses, and he was laughing about how Anglicans had to do courses for everything. But somehow our hands touched as I handed him his coffee. As I looked into his eyes I saw something; longing, warmth, I don't know . . . But we held that gaze for too long.

Come on, Meg. Focus!

I try to imagine this place in summer, and I know it will be lovely. I turn and look at the far side of the bridge. The fine house it led to is long gone. It truly is a bridge leading nowhere. *Hmm.*

I suddenly see something moving in the bushes by the gates. It's an old black Labrador, mooching onto the bridge, followed by a dishevelled-looking man. My keys are in my hand, and I instinctively hold them between my fingers just in case there's trouble – I'm all alone here. But then I see who it is.

Recognition covers his weather-beaten face. I've only spoken to him a few times, a quick hello when I've seen him, usually talking to Barny. I notice today that this unkempt countryman has piercing blue eyes.

'Alright, Miss?'

'Hello, Archie! I'm just admiring the view. Isn't it wonderful here?'

'Yep. It's a special place.'

His dog is sniffing at my jeans. I bend down and pat her, noticing as I do so that she is almost blind.

'Come away, Tess,' he tells her.

'It's alright. Anyway, I have to go.'

'Say 'ello to Arthur for me,' he says, as I walk past him. ''E's a good sort, but 'is wife's a bit iffy.'

I laugh. *Yeah, and you're on her list, so you'd better watch out!*

'She were at school with me, in the village, back in the day. A bit older, mind.'

'What, in Nun's Drift? There isn't a school in—'

'Nah, all us kids went to St Mary's in Fall's End. I lives in a cottage between the villages, see, and she lived at the edge of Nun's Drift—' he points, vaguely, 'where that old Co-op is, roundabouts. She's in one of them posh bungalows now, ain't she, since she married Arthur? Nice bloke.'

'Very nice,' I smile.

'Yeah, we all used to play 'ere, years ago. When we was young . . .' His voice quietens to silence.

I cast one long look over my shoulder; he's standing on the bridge staring at the quiet lake, dog sitting patiently at his side. He seems to belong here, somehow.

That evening, I'm having dinner with Rosemary and Arthur. He's wonderful; he never complains, even when Rosemary is being too exuberant, always has a twinkle in his eye, and a gentle, dry humour. The other guest is Alexandra Thompson-Tracey. It's a put-up job, of course; engineered so we can *do good* to her, and I can get to know her better. *Oh joy.* Still, I readily accepted the invitation; it got me out of attending Jason's Friday night study group at the vicarage. Rosemary thinks I'm very noble, sacrificing the meeting 'on the only night Ally can make it'. (*Really*?) Little does she know!

'Rosemary knew my mother,' Ally's saying in her cut-glass accent, dolloping potatoes onto her plate from the dish.

'Yes, I knew that. I'm sorry about . . .'

'No need to be sorry, sweetie, all too long ago. Potatoes? Or are you dieting?' *How rude!* 'Arthur knew her too, didn't you, my darling?'

'Yes, she was fun. Didn't have bad legs, either.' Arthur winks at Ally, whose perfect, mask-like face cracks into a slight smile.

I reach for the dish with the peas in it, ladling them on between the mashed potato and the slices of succulent lamb.

'So, Ally . . .' I try to sound interested. 'How're the horses?'

'Well, much the same as they've always been,' she replies, breezily. 'Quite large, leg at each corner, tendency to flatulence, that sort of thing.'

What's the point! I slosh a load of Rosemary's delicious gravy over my food and don't pass Ally the gravy boat.

'And you,' she says, glancing at me. 'How's that little chap you're dating?'

Little chap! He's six foot two! He also told her he wasn't interested, when she flirted with him – or so he says – so I know what's happening here.

I say, coolly, 'Barny's not my chap, we're not dating, but he's fine, as far as I know.'

'He's been to Kent to see his father, hasn't he?' Arthur offers me honey-glazed carrots.

'Thank you, yes. He was in hospital with a suspected heart attack.' I glance up and see Rosemary pursing her lips. She *really* doesn't like Barny. 'Heartbreaker!' she's said to me. 'It's written all over him!'

Possibly, but it's in his past. He's trying to change. And besides . . . All these conflicting emotions!

'He did some work for me last summer.' Ally picks up her knife and fork. Her smooth brow wrinkles into a slight frown. 'At least, I *think* it was him. Anyway, it was some tradesman . . .'

Oh, you know it was him alright! I stare at my plate, grimly, and then Rosemary announces that we should say Grace. Ally seems amused. Rosemary says a brief prayer of thanks to God, and I instantly feel ashamed for not being nicer when I'm meant to have faith in a Good Shepherd who loves everyone. Even Ally.

'Would you like some mint sauce?' I say, when Rosemary has finished her prayer. Ally shakes her head, her dark ponytail bobbing. Her clear grey eyes are shrewd and mildly contemptuous.

'So, do you still go riding with the vicar?' asks Arthur, brightly. 'Talk of the village, you know.'

My heart lurches.

Ally laughs like one of her horses – loud and whinnying. 'Really? Yes, we go for a hack sometimes, helps poor old Jason relieve some of his stress, you know.' She smirks, and chomps away on her hay and oats – sorry, peas and lamb. 'He just *loves* Chosen Hill.'

'He's a lovely man,' gushes Rosemary. 'It's such a pity . . .'

'Pity he isn't married?' Ally says, lifting her face out of her nosebag. 'Oh yes, but he's made this ridiculous vow, hasn't he? Some religious stuff. You know, lifelong celibacy, all that nonsense.'

'I'd say it's a massive sacrifice, wouldn't you?' I feel my face flush. She smirks again as our eyes meet. *She knows.*

'Oh, he'd forget all that rubbish if he had the right woman.' Ally dabs her mouth delicately on her napkin. 'He's not a bad rider, though, I'll give him that. Actually, I've often thought he has a *wonderful* seat.'

Rosemary starts to cough – she's apparently swallowed some peas the wrong way. I've lost my appetite. I push my half-empty plate away. 'Meg's looking after Ally.' *No, she's not!*

'Why don't you girls have a nice talk while we clear up?' Rosemary stares at me pointedly as she leans across and takes my plate. 'I'm sure you've got a lot in common.'

The only thing we have in common is our taste in men.

Ally pushes her chair back while Rosemary organises Arthur in the kitchen.

'She's wrong,' she comments, bluntly.

'Well,' I say, making a monumental effort to sound cordial. 'I don't ride, for a start.'

Her lip curls. 'No. I don't suppose you do.'

Silence . . . punctured only by lots of clattering from the kitchen and Rosemary telling Arthur off.

I fix my eyes on some of Rosemary's twee china on the Dutch dresser opposite me – little dogs with their paws up in prayer. Rosemary likes her dressers – she has one in the kitchen, and this darker one with the oval top in the dining room. Plates, jars, cups, all rosy. But my eyes are fixed on the little dogs and I wonder what they're praying for. For me to find a good excuse to go home? Possibly. But Rosemary really wants me to befriend this hard-faced shrew; and so, apparently, does Jason!

I have a sudden thought. 'Do you know anything about the bridge at Fall's End?'

Ally raises her well-plucked eyebrows. 'Oh – yes. Right on the edge of our land.'

Thanks for reminding me.

'Why d'you want to know?'

'Well, I—'

'Used to be a big house there, but I don't remember it.' She sits back in her seat, not at all fazed by the fact that she's just interrupted me. 'Got bombed or something in the war. But it was already derelict – last used by some priests, I think. Pretty secluded, if you don't mind the ghosts.'

'Ghosts?'

Another smirk. Can't this woman smile properly? 'Not afraid of them, are you? The past tends to hang around.' Her voice sounds brittle. 'Always with us. Yes?'

'Not necessarily.' I'm tired of her company. 'I think we can let go and choose to move on.'

'Oh, can we?'

'Yes,' I say, firmly. 'We can learn to live with past mistakes.'

'I didn't say anything about mistakes,' she shoots back.

I raise my voice. 'Rosemary, do you want a hand?'

She pops her head round the door and beams. 'No, dear. I'll bring the trifle in, in a minute.'

Ally is scrolling through her phone. I study her face with dislike. But then, in an instant, as if someone has pointed to something I hadn't noticed before, I see it; for all her money and privilege and horses and whatever else, she's sad. I feel an unwanted wave of compassion. *OK, one more go.*

There's a box on the table. I take a mint, and push the box towards her. 'Have one.'

She looks up. 'I don't eat chocolate that's less than 70 per cent cocoa solids. Not great for your teeth *or* your weight, you know.'

I bite into the mint. *Why is life so difficult?*

It's Saturday morning, and I'm meant to be checking on stuff to do with my new car. It's just an excuse, really. Rosemary's covering me at work again, and I need to get back to the café. But instead, I'm at the bridge at Fall's End. Why? I don't know. Maybe the mystery's a bit of a distraction.

There's that now-familiar sense of the trees just holding their breath . . . waiting for some divine permission to 'go!' before they explode into life.

It's so beautiful here. Cold today; I've got my green padded jacket on, and my eyes are watering. My phone is switched off.

A lone moorhen chirrups, and pushes its way across the still water. I reflect; since I came to live in Nun's Drift nearly a year ago, my life has changed. I need to count my blessings, practise gratitude, as Rosemary so often reminds me.

I've tried to find out about this bridge, and the house it led to; there's not much online. But I did discover that Ally was right; there's some daft rumour about mysterious, disappearing shades of a man and a woman being seen here in the twilight, years ago. Ghosts? Who knows.

Footsteps on the bridge. My heart skips a beat. Archie! *Not stalking me, is he?* His elderly dog comes up, wagging its tail.

'I'm here again,' I say, somewhat pointlessly.

'Looks like it.' Archie narrows his eyes as he looks across the lake.

Make an effort, Meg. After all, Archie's one of the people Rosemary thinks we ought to be nice to. 'I hear there are ghosts.'

'Oh, I don't hold with that.' I'm surprised at the forcefulness of his tone. 'And neither would the vicar, I shouldn't think.'

The vicar. My heart turns over. 'Oh . . . You don't believe in spiritual stuff, then?'

'I never said that,' he replies, gruffly. 'But I don't hold with spooks. What's gone is gone, I reckon, and leave all that to him upstairs.'

I certainly didn't expect to get a mini-spiritual lecture from this man.

He looks at me sideways. 'So, how's your young fella, then? That Barny? Always chats. Ain't seen him around much – he does all the paintin' and decoratin' and takin' care of the churchyard, don't he? Odd jobs, like?'

It occurs to me that the only person I have ever seen Archie talking to is Barny.

'Oh – he's been visiting his father. Yes, he's – well, Barny's a carpenter. And he's not my fella. We're – er – friends.'

He's looking at me quite intently, with those very blue eyes, and I feel a little disconcerted. Then he half-smiles, shoves his hands in his pockets, whistles to his dog, sniffing at the other side of the bridge, and wanders away.

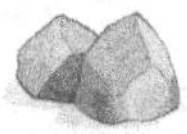

'Hey!' Barny really is good-looking, with his slightly crooked smile. I'm in the café, just shutting up shop, and Rosemary is doing something in the kitchen. 'Is your phone still off? If I didn't know better, I'd think you were avoiding me.'

'I've been really b—' That's a lie. I haven't been *that* busy.

Rosemary appears, pulling on her elegant black gloves. 'I'm off now. Oh!'

Her eyes lock with Barny's. These two have absolutely no love for each other, or even an iota of liking. He stands away, hands hipped. For a moment I have a great surge of feeling for him. Moody, troubled, gorgeous . . . how can I tell him I don't want anything other than friendship?

'Sometimes,' he comments, as Rosemary grabs her fake fur hat and says a curt 'goodbye', 'I really fancy a smoke.'

'Well done you for giving up.' I pull out one of the chairs, scraping it on the tiled floor.

'Well, I haven't really. Just cut down.' He fixes me with a serious stare. 'It's hard giving up something you want.'

He sits, then, and puts his elbows on the table. My mouth goes dry. I could do with a cigarette, too.

'What's going on, Meg?' His voice is low as he leans forward. 'I thought you and I were – well, I thought there was . . .'

I take a deep breath. 'Look, I'm not feeling it, OK?'

He sits back, clearly stunned. I guess he doesn't get turned down by women too often.

'I'm sorry,' I say. 'I mean, we didn't even kiss. We're friends, right? It wasn't a real relationship.' *Quick, Meg, think of something! Don't hurt him.* 'I'm just not ready for anything more.' *Liar.*

He gets up, and his face, usually pretty unreadable, is lined with disappointment.

'I'm sorry,' I repeat. 'I suppose I'm—' *I suppose I'm in love with the vicar.*

Shocked at my own thoughts, I'm silenced, but it doesn't matter. He doesn't hear me anyway. The doorbell tinkles, he's gone.

I promised myself, and maybe God, that I would never hurt anyone again. Ally talked about the past, but my past is full of hurting people and selfishness. I had an affair with my best friend's fiancé. I hated myself for what I did, the guilt, the disgust at my own weakness, and it's taken me a long time to get over that.

I go upstairs to my little bedroom. *It had to be done. I couldn't string him along.* But I did like him; I just didn't want a 'relationship', that's all.

I sit on my bed. *You know what? Jason has it all sorted. Be celibate and single, do good to people but keep your distance. Fix your eyes on the Good Shepherd. Nothing else!*

There's a noise. A WhatsApp message – from Jason! I lie back on the rose-patterned duvet. It's a group message, church, something to do with Lent. I don't know anything about the Church calendar, it's all new to me. Just like faith. I've been learning that Lent is about giving something up.

Well, I just did, didn't I?

The uplifting missive he's put on WhatsApp is about letting go of the past. Letting go of things that are wrong in your life so there's room for something new.

Jason! I chuck the phone down on the bed. *It's impossible. A road – a bridge, maybe – to nowhere.*

I fall into a troubled sleep, wake up, undress, go back to bed then sleep till dawn.

The next morning the weather is bright.

It's Sunday. Church. But even with all that sleep, I'm not feeling great; just groggy.

Do I go? Or not? What else have I got to do? At least I'll see people.

I drag on my boots and head for St Saviour's, puffing up the hill like an oldie. Good job I gave up smoking. I determine to get more exercise.

I'm crunching along the gravel path, looking at the gravestones, and the wind is blowing my hair around. I really need to get it cut.

'Archie! That old scruffbag?'

I recognise the clipped tone, and see Ally in the porch, with Rosemary. Ally doesn't usually 'do' church. She's wearing a blue gilet and tight jeans; slim and trim.

'You won't like this, Rosemary, but honestly, I so wouldn't bother.'

Rosemary's all pink wool and beige trousers. 'Well,' she's saying, 'I don't agree. Everyone's—'

Ally, so good at interrupting, waves a hand dismissively. 'My advice is, don't waste your time.'

I can see Rosemary spluttering some sort of reply. I'm not in the mood to back her up, so I cast her an ironic look, say nothing and walk into the ancient church, already filling with worshippers. Jason draws a good crowd.

I choose my usual seat by the stained-glass window of the Good Shepherd. I shut my eyes. Someone sits down beside me and I can tell by the overpowering floral scent that it's Rosemary. I keep my eyes closed.

There's a noise. I look up to see a man's hand on the back of the pew in front.

'Good morning, ladies.' Jason's rather pointedly smiling at Rosemary. I'm suddenly aware that my hair must look a complete mess, and attempt to smooth it down. I glance across the aisle and see Ally standing there watching me with a mocking smile.

'Vicar! Can I borrow you later?'

'Oh – er – yes, Rosemary! About . . .?'

'Passion, Vicar!'

He seems flustered. 'Er – what?'

'The Easter Passion Play! I was telling Meg, it's quite a thing . . . it starts off at Fall's End, and finishes up in

Nun's Drift. It's a massive undertaking, isn't it? Lots of preparation. All run by the wonderful Rev Kathy. I'm hoping to give out some leaflets—'

Ally is shifting herself along to sit by Rosemary and interrupts the flow.

'Hello, Jason,' she says, warmly.

'Hey, Ally.' The reply is warm, too, and I feel an unexpected surge of jealousy. 'I wonder where Barny's got to?' Jason goes on. 'I thought he'd be here but I haven't seen him.'

'Ask Meg – she'll know,' Ally says, quickly.

I focus on the flagstones.

Rosemary's voice breaks through the tension. 'Flora says he isn't feeling well.'

Oh, I wish I hadn't come.

I usually like listening to Jason, but today he talked more about Lent – giving something up – and it made me feel unsettled. He was telling a story about a man carrying a load of bricks in a rucksack along a difficult path, then another guy comes alongside, carrying a similar rucksack, and says, 'Why are you carrying those bricks when I'm carrying them for you?' And the second bloke's the Good Shepherd . . .

'Got to let go, people,' Jason had said. 'Let go of the past, that problem, whatever it is that holds you. Let *him* carry it and work it out. OK?'

So, do you do that, then, Jason? Am I a problem to be 'let go of', or don't you see it that way?

I remember my fine words to Ally, at Rosemary's place, all that stuff about moving on and choosing to let the past go. Yes, I believe I've done that. But . . . old patterns, old thoughts; new thoughts that play into old patterns – what about them?

Leaving the church, I dodge Jason's awkwardly proffered hand and walk to the old wall. I perch there, staring out at fields just glazed with green. The stone is cold, and for a moment I wish it was the broken, winsome stone of the forlorn bridge at Fall's End, because that's just how I feel.

I swivel round, and gaze at the castle-like church. There's nothing to commend it, it's not beautiful. But it's solid and dependable; you can trust it, somehow. It doesn't matter what it looks like on the outside. Inside, there's warmth and acceptance, like home; and it's a fortress, a bastion against the battering winds of life.

The worshippers are leaving, walking away through the myriad dead people buried under the green grass and scattered primroses. *Life is so short.*

I've already travelled quite a distance on my own emotional journey; certainly since last May, when I arrived here anxious and weighed down by poor decisions. I feel as if I've grown as a person, discovering faith. Such a challenge, and quite scary – seeing myself more clearly in the mirror of Someone's perfect life. But, like the start of a new chapter, inviting, exciting, with the promise of the unexpected.

What if you've only been into this faith thing because you fancy the vicar?

I consider the thought. Well, Jason certainly does make faith very appealing. But surely that's not the reason!

I hear voices, and see Rosemary, Ally and Jason talking by the porch. I turn and stare at the blue sky for a while, and when I glance over my shoulder, everyone's gone.

The wind is chill, and I decide to head towards my favourite seat by the wall. It's sheltered there.

Come on, Meg. Barny will be OK. Jason's your friend, he's in your life, you've lost nothing. And the faith thing . . . it's real. Or becoming real. Isn't it?

As I reach the bench, I suddenly catch sight of a metal disc on the back of the seat, glinting in the spring sunshine. They're often dedicated to someone, benches, aren't they? So why have I never thought about this one before? I look: *In loving memory: Elizabeth Thompson-Tracey*, and some dates that indicate that she was only in her forties when she died. Ally's mother. Of course.

How difficult it must have been for Ally, away at boarding school, and coming home, her father bereaved, and then seeing him quickly marry again . . . No wonder she's got this reputation for being so arrogant. Maybe it's all a front. Perhaps there's a vulnerable young girl in there somewhere. Another wave of compassion for her.

I hear tuneless whistling. It's the churchwarden, ambling along the path.

'Afternoon, Meg!' he says, stopping as he sees me. 'We've got a snake around . . . probably just a grass snake, don't suppose it's an adder, but you never know. I wonder if Barny's seen it when he's been working here? Do you know where he—'

'No! I really don't!' I get up and swiftly walk into the church, away from the wide-eyed churchwarden.

This space has always felt so safe to me; there's no condemnation here. I feel tears pricking my eyelids. I'm standing near the stained-glass Good Shepherd; I look up, seeing the little lamb in his arms, blurry as the tears spill onto my cheeks.

My voice is broken, edgy. 'Why isn't life just full of happiness and no problems?' I swallow the lump in my throat. 'Why's there always *stuff*?'

No answer.

Did I expect one?

It's just a window, after all.

I feel a sudden sense of futility sweep over me. Then, slowly, slowly, I begin to tangibly feel the peace of the sanctuary and I find myself surrendering to a quietness that seems to not quite belong to this earth. Light shines through the stained glass, and the colours appear richer and bolder than I've ever known them.

'I can't carry this load!' My voice sounds loud in the empty building. 'You know what? I don't think I even know what the load is!'

You don't have to name every brick in the backpack, Meg.

Who said that? A little voice in my mind, my heart?

I sit down in the nearest pew, and bow my head as tears fall on my jeans. And I see it. It's not a once-in-a-lifetime deal. This moving on and letting go is ongoing. Maybe that's what Jason meant in his talk; that we need to constantly let go just to take the next step – if we want to go forward in life, in faith. Perhaps it's not even knowing what the *stuff* is, at times; the dead ends, the hurts, the wrong turns, the things that don't make sense, the disappointments, those heavy bricks we carry, each one weighing us down and making the load more difficult to bear . . . Maybe all the Good Shepherd is asking of us is that we trust him that he understands.

I don't know.

Eventually, I leave the church. I see the churchwarden wielding a watering can. He eyes me warily as I approach.

I put my hand up. 'I'm so sorry. About earlier, I mean.'

'That's alright,' he shrugs.

'I hope you find your snake.'

He chuckles. 'There's always a serpent in Paradise, isn't there?'

'I suppose there is.' I smile and walk away.

I know nothing's really sorted, but I feel lighter. Letting go of things that are just too heavy for me . . . that's a challenge. But if Someone bigger than me wants to carry my bricks, I'm going to let him.

I suppose that's faith, or trust, or hope, or maybe all three. But I know I can't carry this load called 'life' alone.

Maybe knowing that is enough.

I guess, for now, it will have to be.

PART TWO

Barny's Story

Choices and Control

Lying back, hands clasped behind my head. *Rebound relationships never work, Barny.* I shut my eyes. *Relationship! Don't be ridiculous. It's a distraction. And anyway, who wants it to work?*

I remember what happened today.

I was fixing a couple of shelves at *Bellwood's Antiques.* The old bat who runs it was sitting on a wobbly chair behind the counter, in a dark coat and felt hat, glaring. The daughter walked in – again. It was her day off, apparently; she works in the charity shop in Fall's End, but Tuesdays, she's at the antiques place, with her mother telling her what to do.

Paula Bellwood is not the greatest beauty in the world. Older than me by several years, dark hair, tall, skinny body, never looks happy. But one bright smile and a knowing wink and she was falling over herself to fetch me the biscuits.

I was just getting my pay when she said, 'We've got a few problems at the charity shop. There's a sort of leak in the lean-to at the back.'

'You probably need a sort of plumber, then,' I'd replied, lightly, looking at my phone, but raising my eyes, eventually, to see her reaction . . . More colour in her face than I'd seen before.

'Are you going to pay him, Paula?' the mother had snapped. Paula had glanced at her, with clear irritation.

'Well, what do you think, Barny? Can you take a look?'

I'd shrugged, pretended I wasn't sure. 'Well, you know, I'm not a plumber.'

'I'm sure you could just take a look at it, Barny, there's a problem when it rains, that's all.'

Begging. I like that.

'Hmm . . . can do later tomorrow, OK? I'll just have a quick look, can't promise anything.'

'He hasn't given you an exact time, Paula!' the mother pointed out. I remember thinking, *Can't this old dragon speak to me? Why does she only speak to her daughter?*

'Doesn't matter,' Paula replies. 'Thank you, Barny!'

Now, I'm lying on my bed, and I really fancy a smoke. But Mrs F – I'm her lodger – doesn't like smoking in the house and anyway, I was giving it up. I thought it would impress Meg. So much for that!

My landlady's banging plates around in the kitchen. A pleasant smell drifts up the stairs. I sigh.

Mrs F's homemade lasagne and garlic bread is always delicious, but I don't have an appetite. It's just a few days since Meg told me she didn't want to know, but it seems like forever. I feel a rising anxiety in my chest. *Nobody gets to me like this.*

'Barny! Dinner's ready.'

'Not hungry, Mrs F!' I call.

I groan as I hear the stairs creaking. Mrs F, a sixty-something widow and really sweet, knocks on my door. She's coming in. I sit up.

'Barny, are you still off-colour?'

'No,' I say, feeling like a kid. 'I'm alright.'

'Well, you're clearly not, are you?'

I stand up and stretch and decide it's time to lie. 'I ate something when I was out. I'm all good.'

She frowns. I can see she's not convinced. Time to turn on the charm.

'Look, thanks for worrying about me, but I really am OK. Just tired. That old – I mean, Mrs Bellwood – is pretty demanding, you know.'

'How's your dad?'

Whoa! Didn't expect that. I run a hand through my hair.

'Doing OK, thanks.' I'm good at shutting down feelings. I drove away from Dad's and did what I usually do: lock the past up in a box and don't open the lid.

'Hmm. Well, I'll put your dinner in the oven, but don't wait too long. It'll dry up.'

'OK. I appreciate it.' As she closes the door, I wish she hadn't been so kind. I shut my eyes. My feelings for my father are manageable. Well – I just don't look at them. That's the way it's been since I was about fifteen.

Block out the hospital bed, the frailty, the scared old bloke that I just see as a sad man who got tearful and threw out Bible verses as well as vomit when he was drunk.

I don't want to think of the hand stretched out to me that I grasped briefly but couldn't hold. *Nah. I don't do emotion.* Anyway, he's getting better. Forget about all the cloying need, leave that for his sister to deal with.

But Meg . . . I didn't mean for her to get to me. *No one* gets to me. I just can't get this feeling locked down, locked up, however much I try.

I see a picture in my mind. Meg, at the pub, in the hallway between the back door and the men's loo. Big mirror there, full body, and she's leaning forward applying lipstick or lip salve or whatever it is girls use. *Wow* . . .

What did I do wrong? Tried to push her into something I wanted and she didn't? She seemed to like me, although on reflection, she was always a bit cool, kept her distance; that was quite a turn-on. She never let me kiss her. So . . . she was a challenge. Just thought she was keeping me waiting because she was into religion now – purity, all that stuff. Still: I didn't think she *actually* meant she just wanted to be friends; I thought she'd give in—

Meg, with that long wavy chestnut hair and green eyes that twinkle. Can't believe it was *me* she rejected. *You know, I've noticed the way she smiles at Old Dazzles – Jason. Surely she can't* . . . I push that thought away. A chunky vicar who wears old-fashioned sweaters and doesn't seem to know what he's doing most of the time – she'd prefer *that* to me? No way.

I wonder if jealousy will do the trick.

I'm coming out of Mrs F's the next day when I hear a voice.

'What ya doin', then, mate? Ain't seen you around.'

'Oh, hi, Archie.' I glance up at him as I unlock the van. He's just appeared on the pavement, old dog on a rope lead as ever. 'I'm fine, thanks.' *I'm not.*

'Gonna rain. I hope your next job's indoors.'

I like this old boy, but right now, I don't want to talk. 'Yep, just going to price a job,' I say, with a tight smile. 'In Fall's End.' Don't know why I'm volunteering the information. It's none of his business.

'Seen your young lady down there,' he says. My heart skips a beat.

'Oh yeah, and what young lady's that, then?'

'The one with all that nice red-brown hair. She was on the bridge over the lake. Don't look very 'appy either, if you ask me.'

'I didn't,' I point out, as I open the driver's side door, but my heart flips over. 'See you soon.' *Is she missing me?* A surge of sudden hope.

I get in the van and start the engine.

I park outside the rundown little shops in the 'market square' in Fall's End. A couple of old dears walk past, glancing at me sideways. I notice a red sports car – Daisy Parker comes out of the pharmacist's.

'Oh, hello, Barny!' she says; her accent is nearly as posh as Ally Thompson-Tracey's. 'What're you up to?'

Why do people always want to know my business?

'Work.' I stare up at the heavy grey skies. 'Gonna rain,' I say. 'Better get on.' I glance at her as she gets into the old MGB GT. Classic car, classy lady. Must be late forties, but pretty fit. And quite a cheeky smile.

I walk towards the charity shop. I see movement in the window behind a headless dummy wearing a cream jumper and shiny necklace. Paula is waiting for me. I remember the flush in her cheeks when I'd asked for her phone number almost as a second thought as I'd left her mum's shop yesterday.

I go in, forcing the old door, which seems to stick. I see a rack of used clothes that someone has tried to spruce up to sell, and some ornaments and books on shelves. There's a musty smell, like a jumble sale in a damp old church hall. I lean against the counter, noticing some pictures on the wall, gaudy flowers in badly painted pots. 'So . . . what can I do for you?'

I get a kick out of the blushing and I feel a very familiar tightening in my chest. I can almost feel my heart hardening. Then I remember my dad. Suddenly I don't feel quite as confident. My dad had a heart attack . . .

'Um – the rain comes in,' says Paula, a little breathlessly. 'Let me show you.'

We walk through the shop to a little storeroom, a dressing room, and then past an alcove where there's a kettle and a sink. There's a lean-to, plastic roof; looks like it was cobbled together by some amateur years before.

It started raining now, and the water is hammering on the roof. I hear it . . . drip drip drip. I soon find the leak; yes, I can fix that. A quick trip to the hardware store and I'll be done. Out of nowhere I feel the anxiety gathering in my chest again; I have to get out. I mumble something to Paula, and walk outside of the stifling, dark place with its smell of old clothes, and the shelves that seem to close in on me.

I take a few deep breaths, letting the rain, light now, wash my face.

Disappointment. Loneliness.

Lots of young mums in SUVs picking up their kids from the Victorian building over the road . . . St Mary's School. I've been asked to do some work there, the end of this week. So, it looks as if I'm around for a bit. I'm so used to moving on, and I know the best thing would be for me to get away – forget. *But if you do that, you'll never see Meg again. Will you?*

'So,' I say, as I finish the repair. 'You ever heard of a bridge in this village?'

I look up at her. She's towering over me. I'm crouching down, packing my stuff away. I notice she's put some make-up on. Mascara, with some eyeliner. Her eyes look dark and predatory.

'There's some bridge over a lake, isn't there?' I repeat.

'Oh yes . . . Used to lead to an old priory or something but that's gone. Kids used to play there but they say it's haunted so – well. You know . . .' She seems to run out of words as I stand.

'So, whereabouts is this place, then?'

'Huh? Oh – past the garage, take a right – Howfield Lane. Path opposite the church, by a layby. You can see the lake from . . .' I'm standing too close to her and enjoy her nervousness. Her face is totally readable. Just for a second, I'm tempted . . .

It's no use. I can't.

'OK, just the charge for the bits, and an hour's work. OK?' I pick up my stuff and sidestep her.

She follows me. I can't wait to get out of that shop. She fumbles around in the till, says she hasn't got the exact amount, and asks if I want payment in cash or straight to my bank account. The latter, thanks. *Just do it.*

'We've got a few problems with the stairs,' she says, as I turn to leave. 'I think the top step's a bit dangerous. Would you like to look at it?'

I say, 'Got to be somewhere at four.' *Yeah, on my own, in my van, having a smoke.*

I get out of there as fast as I can. *Barny, you're losing your touch.*

I sit in the van for a moment, wiping a hand over my face. *So anxious.*

It occurs to me that I could talk to Old Dazzles about this. *No.* I start the van. Where's this bridge?

I turn out of the market square, trying to remember Paula's instructions.

I park in the layby and start along the path. I curse, because my feet are getting wet – trainers are not made to get muddy, and the path leading to this mystery bridge isn't the easiest to navigate. Halfway across a field, I want to turn back. I don't suppose Meg will be there, standing looking at a lake in the rain. But I feel compelled to go on.

I find the bridge at last. No Meg, though.

I walk to the centre, and turn to the left, staring over a surprisingly large expanse of water. Drops of rain make many circles in it, and I don't know why I feel so fascinated by that. *Come on, Barny, you've seen rain before.* But it feels therapeutic and calming.

For a moment I'm tempted to get too close to the edge, and wonder how deep the reeded lake actually is. With a shaking hand I get my cigarettes and lighter out.

Seems incongruous somehow to do something so wholly unhelpful, really, in the middle of all this tranquillity. I light the cigarette – I can't smoke it. I let it fall into the water and feel as if I've defiled it.

I want to run away. Run away from these feelings of disappointment. Of rejection. The irony hits me, though – how many women have *I* rejected? How much disappointment have *I* caused? The phone calls I haven't returned; the girls I've made such a point of pursuing, then coolly walked away from.

I deserve this loneliness. I can't even show my dad I love him.

Oh, God. Is that a prayer? I remember my mum leaving. Nothing's hurt me like that until now. It's like the weight of years bearing down on me.

'Oh, God!' Now it *is* a prayer, and I vocalise it. I squeeze my eyes shut, blocking out the view. 'Oh, God!'

I don't know how long I stand like that, but when I open my eyes, the rain has stopped and there's a shaft of sunlight brightening the late afternoon sky as the clouds roll slowly away.

The brightness seems to hit the lake, and there are sudden sparkles on the water. Somehow, there's peace, just for a minute or two. Real peace.

Then I remember something Old Dazzles said a while back. He was talking with the group over in the nondescript town of Fairleigh – a few guys, we get together for snacks and a chat; not that I've been lately, with Dad and Meg, all that. Anyway, we were talking about life, and the consequences of our actions, and I'd said something, light-heartedly, about not having to face any consequences if you just choose to check out, leave.

Of course, that started quite a debate. One of the fellas was saying his daughter's boyfriend just left her with a baby, so he started to get pretty angry. I sat back and let him vent; I saw his point but he was so aggressive. I wondered if his daughter was aggressive too and that was the reason the lad walked out. Didn't dare say it.

'OK, let's think about this.' Dazzles broke into the conversation in his measured, even voice. He looked thoughtful as he took off his glasses – wears specs now to read; he says he's getting old – old! He's only a little bit older than me. When everyone was quiet, he went on, thoughtfully, 'So, if you don't face the consequences of your actions, a couple of things happen, right? Someone else has to face them. And it becomes a lifestyle, so eventually, you're out of options – you're face to face with it, no way out.'

'Not if you run real fast,' I'd shot back.

Jason didn't seem to be fazed by my answer. *Would love to see this guy lose control. Surely he must sometime, somewhere, somehow?*

'Facing situations is how you grow, though,' he'd said. 'If you run from them and never address them, you just fall into the same old pattern of dealing with stuff and it never gets resolved. And one day you're going to hit a wall.' He had cake crumbs down his front. Definitely overweight. I'm thinking now . . . *Meg likes this guy? Never! She can't . . .*

'I believe in free will, though,' I'd said, defensively. 'Got to be in control, and—'

'Why?'

Why? It was a stupid question. Why!

I came out of that house wondering why I bothered to go in the first place. Unfortunately, I was giving Dazzles a lift. I was really irritated with him. He must have known that because he kept quiet all the way back to Nun's Drift. It was only when I pulled up at the vicarage to let him out that he turned in his seat and spoke.

'Barny, you really can't control life. Stuff happens. People do things, say things, and it affects us. You need to let go.'

It was like something he said at one of his daft meetings on a Friday evening. I went to the one last Friday, made an excuse and left. Boring, irrelevant stuff about giving things up. As if that helps. Anyway, Meg hadn't been there. Probably because she was working out how to tell me she wasn't interested the next day.

I'm doing a little job at the vicarage, and Jason isn't around. Maybe he's visiting someone, I don't know, but I'm relieved I don't have to listen to any more of his vicar waffle for a while. I'm in the kitchen, sorting out some broken floor tiles, and Mrs F – who does some 'chores' for Dazzles – is rather annoyingly stepping around me.

'Could you just stay outside the kitchen for a bit?' I say at last, exasperated.

She's hesitating. I suspect she has something to say that isn't related to floor tiles. I lean back against a cupboard.

'Come on,' I say, resigned. 'Let's have it.'

'You were with Paula Bellwood yesterday, weren't you?'

'What? Oh – did a job for her. So?'

Mrs F shifts around a bit. 'Er . . . Paula's mother thinks – well . . .'

I get up and turn my back on her, gazing out of the window; there are poplars in the distance, standing tall and barely green on the edge of the village; and, in the vicar's garden, the blossom is just appearing on a few fruit trees. For a moment I feel struck by the beauty of the pink and white buds; it's like a snowstorm, but contained . . .

When I speak, my voice sounds bored. 'I have absolutely no interest in Paula Bellwood. OK?'

Mrs F sounds relieved. 'Oh, good! I *thought* her mother was just being paranoid – she's like that – talk about control! Paula can't go anywhere without her mother wanting to know what time she's coming back. She's thirty-seven! I'm surprised she's still living at home, but of course she had a bit of an issue a few years ago – you know, emotional health.'

I face her. I see the concern – and the warning – in her expression.

I don't say anything. I get down on the floor again. *This place. These women. Vicars telling you what to do. Why am I still here?*

I've sent her a message. As soon as I did it, I wished I hadn't. Looks needy. Looks desperate. *Hey, Meg, how you doing?* She's doing fine, Barny . . . without you.

I'm at the bridge again. This time I'm not hoping to meet Meg. I just feel drawn here, to the seclusion. Actually, I like Fall's End. If it wasn't for Potty Paula gazing out of her window at me, pretending to rearrange the clothing on that dummy whenever I go to the van, I'd think about getting a room in this village. Nun's Drift is too perfect for me. This village has a grungy garage and a church that's too big for it, a school that looks severe and daunting – and a bridge that leads nowhere. Maybe I need to check out lodgings here. Get away from perfection for a while.

The vicar of Fall's End is a middle-aged, badly dressed woman with short grey hair, no make-up, and a nose ring. She introduced herself to me as I was working in the school with a cheerful, 'Call me Kathy!' The caretaker was off sick, and they need the help of a carpenter in one of the offices. Another job where I'd been recommended by Rev Dazely. I honestly can't get away from that guy doing me good.

Kathy asked me about my availability for a job at her church hall, and we got chatting. I told her I'm thinking of moving out of Nun's Drift. She said there were lodgings in the bungalow next to the King's Arms, so I'd taken a stroll to view the place. Some fella was backing a car out of the driveway onto the main road and glared at me as he did so. He also rolled down the window and shouted that I should move because I was blocking his view. *OK . . . nope.*

I walked back to the school. The dummy in the shop window had changed clothes *again.* I wasn't concentrating; I jumped when I found Paula Bellwood by my van, wearing an unflattering long, grey coat and a multicoloured scarf that looked hand-knitted.

'Oh, Barny, glad I caught you.' She'd pushed a strand of lank dark hair behind her ear. 'What about that little job over the road?'

Please go away.

'Got to make a call.' I'd waved my phone at her, and got in the van. That was when, in a moment of true longing, I messaged Meg. I instantly regretted it. *Stupid!*

The Bellwood woman was standing on the kerb, not moving, staring in my window. She tapped on it. It freaked me out, and I started the engine. I finished up in the layby on the little lane that leads to the Howfields, just as it began to spot with rain.

I never felt any kind of emotion when I heard my dad was ill. I rarely see him. He lives in Rochester, Kent, a fair trip from Suffolk. It was weird going back there; he was always telling me, growing up, about the old days, and the school in Troy Town, where he lived, and the Odeon cinema, long since demolished.

I went for a walk to the castle, then stood looking at the nearby cathedral I recalled so well from my early days. Mum took me; I never knew why, because she wasn't religious. She would talk in low whispers to a man who always seemed to be hanging around outside. She used to tell me to 'go and explore' because she had to tell him something private, but I mustn't tell my dad.

Then she left us.

When I went to see my dad in hospital, I was surprised to feel a tidal wave of anxiety as soon as I walked onto his ward. As I spotted this feeble old guy in the bed, loads of images of him when I was young hit me unexpectedly. So I just thought about Meg, nothing else. It was like if I focused on her, I could cope. Keep those emotions from the past all locked safely away.

Maybe I was focusing on the wrong thing. The wrong person. Maybe I can't focus on anyone. Not even myself.

I'm alone.

Tight feeling in the chest again. I run a hand through my hair. *Life is out of control. Meg hasn't replied to my message. Dad is ill. I've made so many wrong choices.*

I think about God, the Good Shepherd Jason is always going on about. Maybe praying will help. I can't see how; but I remember my earlier desperate attempts – 'Oh, God!' – and finding some measure of peace. OK, truthfully, this Good Shepherd doesn't feel real to me. But I'll try. I don't know what else to do. I can't bear this pain; these acres of hurt inside.

I try to pray, but I can't get any words out. Then I do. But they don't make sense, jumbles of emotions. They fall like raindrops into the lake. Something comes into my mind. I push it away. It appears again. *No. I won't talk to Jason.*

Saturday morning, and I'm in the churchyard trying to locate a snake I don't think exists, and even if it does, is probably never going to harm anyone. There's been a meeting in the church, and a few people are leaking out of it, including Rosemary, who rushes off, probably to the café. Mrs F has told me it was a meeting about this Passion Play they do every Easter, the walk from Fall's End to Nun's Drift, the biggest excitement of the year, apart from the traction engine and old car fair on one of farmer Tony's fields in May.

I can hear Mrs F chatting to someone as she comes out of the church, and glance up to see Kathy Lovell, the minister or vicar or whatever they call them, from Fall's End. She gives me a wave. She's coming over. *Oh no.*

'Hello, young man!' she says, breezily. 'Got a job for you, if you wouldn't mind.' Before I can open my mouth to object, she goes on, 'I need a stone for my empty tomb – something you can easily roll away. Last year we had cardboard and it rained . . . look, can you just knock one up, if I give you the cash for some MDF or whatever? It's got to be quite big – it's got to stand in the entrance to the church.'

'Which church?'

'This church!'

Well, of all the things I have ever been asked to work on, that has to be one of the weirdest.

'Come on, Barny,' she says, brightly. 'You're a carpenter, aren't you?'

'Just like the good Lord,' I say, ironically.

'Barny, you do know you can live different, don't you? You don't have to repeat the old ways of thinking, being.'

'What?'

'What?' she says, her big round eyes looking even rounder. Then I realise it wasn't Kathy who'd made that comment. *I'm hearing voices.* I suddenly wonder if I'm going crazy.

'Nothing. MDF, fake stone? Yeah. Whatever. You've got my number.' I see Old Dazzles coming out of the church and make a decision. 'Excuse me,' I say. 'Jason! Hey! Can I have a word?'

I'm at the hardware store in Fall's End. I really don't need to be here, I spend so much of my time in Screwfix over in Fairleigh, but it's Thursday . . .

I just want to pop in to see Kathy. I have a couple of photos to show her, see if I'm on the right track. OK, so I could have emailed them to her. But it's *Thursday.* Meg comes to Fall's End on Thursdays.

I'm loitering by the window, and then I spot her – the chestnut hair, the green gilet; warm Christmas colours on a cool spring day. She's wandering over to that grinning cheese man, who I can see from here is flirting with her. I clench my fists.

Right, time to make a move.

'Oh, Barny, I *thought* I saw you come in. Have you got time to look at these stairs?'

Paula's behind me! *Stairs? What* – Then I think, *good excuse to be here, to be around, to say hi to Meg . . .*

'Sure, why not?'

I open the door and give her my most charming smile. I hope Meg sees me with Paula. I hope she feels jealous.

I cough loudly, looking at Meg, but she's still chatting to that stupid cheese man. She laughs at something he says. I want to murder him.

'Thanks, Jack!' I shout at the rather startled guy in the hardware store, and slam the door shut behind Paula.

Great! Meg's seen me.

I put my hand in the small of Paula's back as we walk across the square. I catch Meg's eye. Not sure what I see there; uncertainty, confusion – disbelief that I seem to be with Paula?

'Hey, Meg!'

'Oh, hey,' Meg replies, a little guardedly. 'Hello, Paula.'

'Hello.' Paula's voice is cold. 'Come on, Barny, I really want to show you the stairs.'

'Yeah, yeah. Be with you in a moment.' I take my hand away from her back and wander over to Meg.

'How've you been?' I say, casually.

'I'm alright, Barny.' She flicks her hair away from her face. 'Um . . . Didn't see you at church . . .'

'Bit of man flu. I'm OK now.' She glances behind me. I wave at Paula, whose expression is far from happy. 'Hold on a minute, Pauls.'

Paula reddens a little at the shortened version of her name. I look down at Meg. She has such a lovely face, such a beautiful mouth.

'Ah well . . .' *Awkward.* 'See you soon, then.' I turn, and I'm shooting the cheese man what I hope he knows is a warning stare as I stroll over to Paula. I put my arm round her as I move her into her shop. *I so hope Meg is watching this.*

Inside, I quickly look at the stairs. Paula, standing, looking hopeful, is at the foot of the narrow stairwell.

'No, I can't touch this, sorry. Not quite the same as sorting out your leaky lean-to. This building's listed, isn't it?'

'Oh . . . OK, I'll have to talk to . . .'

'Look, what're you doing tomorrow night?'

She stares, as if she thinks she hasn't heard me correctly.

'Are you free? Want to get a drink?'

She coughs and seems embarrassed. 'That would be – ah – yes. OK.'

'I'll pop round for you about nine. Alright?'

'Nine o'clock?'

I don't let the irritation show on my face. How old is this woman? Seven or thirty-seven? *Don't tell me she's in bed by nine!*

'OK, eight-thirty?'

'OK. Yes. I'll – yes. Thank you.'

She is absolutely, 100 per cent flustered. I wonder if she's been on a date, ever.

As I'm going out, I shout back, loudly, 'See you tomorrow night, then, Pauls. OK?'

I look out into the little market square. But there's only the grinning cheese man. No sign of Meg.

Meg often goes to the Half Moon on a Friday, after the church group. She meets her aunt there. I don't care about Bible groups, or whether her aunt is struggling with her partner, or whatever else is going on. What I care about is that Meg is in that pub and sees me with Paula. Am I being childish, playing games? Dunno. But jealousy has worked before with other women.

I get in the van. My phone's ringing. *Jason*! I stupidly told him I'd like to see him to chat, but then changed my mind. He's been after me ever since. I don't answer it, let it go to voicemail.

I turn the key in the ignition and the van roars into life.

The pub is packed. Paula and I are sitting in a window seat, my eyes fixed on the door. She's wearing a really frumpy frock and a knitted grey cardigan. Her hair, straight and dark, lies boringly over her thin shoulders. With every attempt at conversation, I realise we have zero in common. She's clever; she's into books and Shakespearean drama and bands I've never heard of. The talk completely peters out and she gazes mournfully into her apple juice.

I met her as I said I would. She was on the pavement outside the antiques shop, looking back at the place in what I thought was an agitated manner.

'What's up?' I'd said. 'Not scared of the dark, are you?'

She glanced at an upstairs window; there was a dim light in the room, and I saw a shadow moving. Paula put a finger to her lips, and walked away quickly. I followed, glad of the streetlight, because something about that antiques place creeps me out. There was no hiding the resentment in her voice. 'My mother doesn't like me going out in the evening.'

'What are you, a kid?' I shouldn't have said it. She flashed me a look of annoyance, quite visible under the streetlamps.

'She gets frightened on her own.' Paula had stared at me, confrontationally. I could see she was just waiting for me to say something more about her mother.

I didn't risk it. 'OK . . . Half Moon?'

'Are we staying in the village?'

'That's alright, isn't it?' *Quick,* I'd thought, *you need an excuse.* 'Means I can drink, yeah? Don't have to drive.'

'Oh, yes. Of course.' She'd sounded flat.

Good start to the date.

It's quarter to ten. I don't think Meg's going to come in tonight. Her aunt isn't there, but Daisy Parker is. She arrives with a stocky, muscular guy, mixed race and handsome, younger than her – Jack, who runs the hardware store. Still, she's attractive for an older lady, wearing a short leather jacket and well-cut jeans. She runs *Vanity Designs* in the village, and she's a good model for her own – very pricey – clothes.

Paula goes to the loo, and Daisy comes over, leaning on the back of the settle. 'Enjoying yourself, darling?'

'Not so's you'd notice.'

'Surprised to see you with—' She nods in the general direction of the loos, an amused expression on her vivid face. 'Not quite your type, I'd have thought? Anyway, what about our lovely Meg? Not messing her around, I hope.'

'Meg and I are mates, that's all.' I add, coolly, 'Thought she'd be here tonight.'

A perceptive smile graces Daisy's full lips. *Fillers? Who knows.*

'Oh, I see. Well, she's into all this church stuff, isn't she? They're doing Lent. That's all about giving something up, isn't it? Perhaps she's given up the pub. Probably at the vicarage talking about God with the divine Jason.'

That's not something I want to hear.

Paula returns and tries to ignore Daisy, but Ms Parker isn't having any of that.

'Hello, Paula! How lovely to see you! I didn't think you approved of pubs.'

'That's my mother. And I'm not my mother,' comes the surly reply.

Daisy raises her eyebrows and pulls a face at me. Then she moves away with her date.

It seems an age until I can reasonably suggest we leave. We reach the shop, and it occurs to me that I don't want to touch Paula, and have absolutely no desire to kiss her. No chemistry whatsoever. One of the most tedious dates I've ever been on, in fact. But then, she might prove useful when Meg's around. So, as she looks first at her mother's window – light's off – and then at me, in the moonlight, I plant a quick, chaste kiss on her cheek, and say, 'See you soon.'

She fiddles in her handbag for her keys and nods an affirmation. I walk away, leaving her standing outside the little alley that runs round the back of the building.

That evening I get a WhatsApp message. *Thank you for tonight, Barny. It was great! When can we meet again?* I wonder whether she was on a different date to me. Something about that message makes me nervous. *Switch the phone off, Barny.*

She's called me twice by 8 a.m. I block her number, adding hers to the very long list.

Another Saturday morning, and I'm in the churchyard, looking for this ridiculous snake. The churchwarden is convinced it's there, someone else has seen it, and they're scared it's an adder. I think, *Just leave it alone! It's not doing anyone any harm.* I decide I'm going to have a smoke. I reach for my cigarettes and my lighter. So much for giving up.

'Barny!'

I groan, inwardly. 'Oh, hey, Da – Jason.'

I sit down on the nearest bench. Jason sits next to me. I just can't smoke with him sitting there. Annoyed, I put my cigarettes away, and the lighter.

'You wanted to talk to me?' he says.

'Yes. No. Sort of.'

'About your dad?'

'No.'

'Paula?'

I'm startled.

'Come on, Barny, this is Nun's Drift. Everyone knows who was with who in the pub on Friday night.'

I lean forward, arms on my knees. The view from this angle, under a couple of fir trees, is of the sturdy stone church and the clock tower. Impressive. Boring. I don't know.

'What about her?'

'You know she's vulnerable?'

'What are you trying to say?' Something snaps in me and I get up. 'She's a grown woman!' I sound aggressive. He lowers his gaze. This guy used to be into martial arts; he's told me about his past more than once. But now . . . I feel a surge of contempt. *This is the bloke Meg prefers to me, isn't it? This overweight clergyman! Has he even shaved today? Look at him!*

The early April breeze stirs the daffodils nestling beneath the nearby hedge, newly leafed, fresh and bright.

But it's not his fault, is it? You can't make someone love you. You can't control it. It's a free choice. If it wasn't free, then it would mean nothing.

I take a deep breath. I'm not sure those are actually my thoughts. They feel new, somehow. I put a hand to my eyes. What actually is love? I don't know. I don't deal in love. I don't get what it means. I don't understand it. I've never sought it. I've always run . . .

'Paula's emotionally fragile, Barny.'

Yes, I'd guessed that! I take my hand away and find him blinking up at me in the sharp sunshine.

'Look, I'm not interested in Paula! Nothing's happened, OK? I won't see her again, right? I wanted M—' I stop.

Yes – Meg! I wanted her and she didn't want me. Alright? I find it hard to admit it to myself – and realise I certainly can't admit it to Jason.

I sit down on the bench, suddenly deflated. 'My dad's all I've got. He's fifty-eight. That's young, isn't it? Too young to . . . die.' There. I've said it.

He's silent. Then he says, 'What about your mum?'

I reach for my cigarettes. *If he doesn't like it, he can move.* I notice my hand trembling as I light up.

'No idea. You know she left us when I was a kid?' I inhale deeply.

More silence.

I notice the stillness; my hammering heartbeat moves to a steadier rhythm.

I take a last drag of my cigarette. 'You're always saying you can meet your God anywhere. You ever been to that bridge between Fall's End and Nun's Drift?'

'What?' He looks bemused.

'The one spanning the lake.' I stand up again, and grind the cigarette butt into the grass. 'You should go.'

'Why?'

'Much more peaceful than this.' I nod disparagingly towards the church building. 'Meet with your God. That's what you're good at, isn't it?' I hear the bitterness in my voice.

He stands, too. He's nearly as tall as me. I notice that's he's a bit paler than usual. Probably just the effects of winter. *You need some sun, mate.*

'Is it the place he meets with *you*, Barny?'

The question catches me off guard.

I remember my prayers in the rain.

Maybe.

'Catch you sometime, yeah?' I turn and walk away.

I'm by the lake.

Let go, Barny. Let go of things you can't control. It's like Jason is right there with me. I can almost hear his voice.

Only he didn't say that to me, did he? He didn't actually say much at all.

I couldn't stop my mum leaving.

I couldn't make Meg want me.

I hear her 'I'm not feeling it' and think: *How many times have I used that phrase myself?* I briefly think of Paula, and the barely unconcealed bitterness towards her mother – but then, how do I feel about mine?

And then there's my dad. My fear, then my disgust at the way he used alcohol when Mum left. The way he couldn't handle anything. Quoting Bible verses when he was hammered, sick on the carpet, down his vest, and me, just a kid, clearing it up. Me feeling helpless. Me getting out. *Don't look back.* The women were a good distraction.

But now . . .

I'm here facing my worst enemy. *Emotion*.

'God!' I feel utterly lost. Nowhere to hide. Raw, bare, hostility, disappointment, and a whole load of very familiar but forgotten helplessness. Something surges up from somewhere deep inside. I clench my fists and my bellowing, almost animal-like, scream echoes around the lake. 'God! *God*!'

I'm shocked at the force of my own feeling.

I don't know how long I'm there, but eventually I come out of some sort of stupor to find that peace has descended on me like soft rain.

Did I just have a breakdown? Or a meltdown? Is there a difference?

But my mind feels still and clear, like the surface of the lake. I want to stay there forever.

There are some stones by my feet.

I pick one up and wait for a moment.

I toss it into the water. Its entry breaks the stillness.

I watch the disruption.

'You can't control anything, mate,' I murmur. 'Why did you ever think you could?'

PART THREE

Rosemary's Story

Not Judging

I wish I hadn't got involved in this pastoral support thing. I just run a little group of like-minded ladies who want to help the unfortunate souls of our parish. Alright – *I* want to help. Flora Fletcher is ever-patient, doing good just as she goes about her daily life. She's not the sort of person who even needs a list. And I don't think Daisy Parker much cares about anyone other than herself. Bless her. A truly free spirit. The flipside being selfishness. Not that I'm judging. I can't expect much from Meg, either. She clearly doesn't like Ally and the feeling is mutual. So, I feel as if I'm rather bearing the load myself.

I asked Archie Gainsford to do some gardening for us. He does odd gardening jobs, as well as gamekeeping for Jeremy Thompson-Tracey, Ally's father. I came across Archie in the Co-op on Stile Road the other day. Of course, we knew each other as children. He was always a bit eccentric.

I was trying to work his age out as he fixed me with very familiar clear blue eyes. Yes, he was younger than me. Not by much – a year, maybe two. *I'm sixty soon.*

I didn't expect his rather terse reply. I was just noticing he'd brought his old Labrador into the shop, holding it by a rope lead, and the girl on the till was looking very angsty.

'Well, Floss, I'd 'ave thought Arthur could do any work you need, eh?'

I felt myself blanch as I realised he remembered my old nickname. Floss! So much for trying to help.

He paid for his tobacco – I wonder how he affords it, he always looks so poor in his flat cap, dirty jeans and ill-fitting waxed jacket – and wandered out. I stared at the closing door, vexed.

The girl on the till wrinkled her nose and started spraying some kind of scent around the shop. She eyed me knowingly as I bought my kidney beans, and I realised the name 'Floss' would soon be bandied around the village; it took such a long time to bury that monicker and I so want it to stay dead!

I tried to retain some dignity by buying organic butter, but I suspected that even that wouldn't repair my social standing, now that my old nickname had been outed.

It's Tuesday. Meg's going to pick up her new car this morning. She's been a bit low lately, so hopefully this will cheer her up. Next weekend it's Palm Sunday. It's going to be a relaxed church service and I've been asked to do one of the readings. So here I am, in the jolly little café, with all its pretty jugs and bowls and plates, old beams and cosy atmosphere that I love so dearly. It's like a second home, so welcoming. I'm wiping down a table, switching my thoughts from nicknames and butter to donkeys and palm branches, when the door slaps open and in walks a very angry Maureen Bellwood. She looks like an old crow at the best of times, in her wonky felt hat (which she wears indoors) and her black coat. I meet a pair of raven-like eyes and a pointing finger.

'This is your fault!'

'What?' I clutch the cloth to my chest as if it will save me.

'My daughter was in here having a coffee and that womaniser came in and you introduced them. Didn't you!'

I retreat behind the counter, assiduously wiping the surface. I really do not like confrontation. She stalks up. *You know, she really does look like a bird of prey.* I think about offering her a coffee but what the caffeine would do to her in her present state, I dread to think.

'She's disappeared!'

I'm struggling to remember when I might have introduced her daughter to Barny Baines – because I assume it's him she's talking about. I do seem to recall a time, just after Christmas, when Paula was sitting droopily in a corner drinking a mocha, and Barny wandered in. I remember a quick introduction purely because she looked so depressed and I don't like him and wanted to inflict a bit of post-Christmas joy into his world. *I really am a bad person. What's that bit in the Bible about your sins finding you out?* My mother always used to admonish me with that. I'm thinking about it now as Maureen continues.

'Did you hear me, Rosemary? She's gone!'

'Yes. I heard.' I should think the whole of Nun's Drift heard.

Meg appears from the kitchen, wiping her hands on her apron.

'What's up?'

It's ten to nine – I notice the hands on the clock above the door. It's such a nice clock; all flowers and tasteful cathedral hands. Never keeps the proper time. I glance at my watch. Five past . . .

'Oh, so sorry I'm keeping you from whatever's more important than my daughter going missing!'

'What's wrong, Mrs Bellwood?' asks Meg, concerned.

Maureen's voice is rising and I flinch at the shrillness. 'I got up and my daughter wasn't in her bed! I take her breakfast in every morning, and wait . . .' She stands up straight and heaves in a deep breath. Perhaps she feels she's shared too much of their personal life. 'I don't believe her bed has been slept in!' she announces.

I glance at Meg. She's straight-faced.

'Well,' she suggests, 'maybe she stayed overnight with a friend?'

'My daughter,' says the crow, coldly, 'doesn't stay *overnight* with *friends*.'

Lots of words are flitting through my mind. Control being one of them. Weirdness being another.

'Isn't she at work?' Meg offers, tentatively.

'It's her day off!' Maureen shuts her eyes as if she's announcing the worst thing in the world. 'I suspect,' she declares, dramatically, 'that she might be with that awful Baines man.'

'Have you tried messaging her?' If Meg's worried that Barny might have spent the night with Paula, she doesn't show it.

'I called her. She didn't answer.' Maureen purses her already very thin lips.

'I'll message her, if you like,' says Meg. I raise my eyebrows. 'We swapped numbers the other day. I'm trying to source another Welsh spinning chair, and she gets old tat – I mean, old furniture . . .' She stops speaking.

Maureen sinks down on a chair at the nearest table. I pour her a cup of tea and take it to her, silently. She takes a sip, almost absent-mindedly. *I suppose that one's on the house, then.* There's a bleep from Meg's phone and we all jump.

'It's OK,' says Meg. 'She's fine. She says she's gone for a walk.'

'A walk! She's taken the car! When will she be back?' Now there's a hint of desperation in Maureen's voice. 'I need her in the shop,' she adds, rather stiffly. 'I have a doctor's appointment. I'm not well!' I notice her hand is trembling as she reaches for her cup.

Everyone knows Paula is her world. But I suddenly think: *She's got to let go of her, or she'll lose her forever . . .*

'Have a scone.' I nod to Meg, releasing her to get on with her day. She smiles gratefully in return and goes back to the kitchen. I place the scone and a fair portion of strawberry jam in front of Maureen. I half-expect her to start pecking at it. Instead, she pushes the rose-patterned plate away with disdain.

'This kind of cheap pastry upsets my stomach! Anyway – I still blame you, Rosemary, for introducing my daughter to someone wholly unsuitable.' She stands, and any compassion I feel is flushed away like loo paper.

She sweeps out of the shop, and the bell tinkles almost in relief. Meg reappears, looking a little nervous.

'It's alright,' I say. 'She's gone.'

'I'm wondering if we should be worried.' She fishes her phone out of her pocket and reads the message: *'Gone for a walk. Barny doesn't want to see me anymore. Tell my mother I'm never coming back.'*

I bite my lip – yuk; too much cherry lip gloss. 'Oh . . . that doesn't sound good. I suppose I could try calling her later. I've had a few conversations with her . . .' *Yes, over many years, and they were all hard work.*

Meg puts her head on one side. 'Her mum's a bit controlling, isn't she?'

I roll my eyes.

It's half past ten, Meg's aunt has driven her to pick up her car, and comes back to take over from me. I rush home; there are things I want to do. Paula is not in the forefront of my mind, and neither is her mother. I'm thinking of the farm shop and their chilli and chorizo sausages that I really want to get for Arthur's dinner.

Arthur's busy playing chess with old Alec; they do that sometimes, and it keeps them both happy on a rainy day. I put on my rather nice turquoise mac. Arthur has walked to Alec's place, by the Half Moon on the green, and I know they'll be having a pint or two later. I really can't walk all the way to the farm shop in the rain, so I grab the car keys. I'm so grateful Arthur changed our big car for something smaller. I don't much like driving, but I'm relishing the odd bouts of freedom.

I'm just going along Stile Road when I remember I need to get some of that wonderful, special hob cleaner from the hardware store in Fall's End. Might as well go there while I've got the car.

I park outside the farm shop, am tempted to buy more of their products, then head off towards the next village. I expect to see Meg whizzing past me in her new vehicle, but there are no other cars on the road. The windscreen wipers start their steady thump, thump, thump as the rain is wiped away.

I'm just about to drive past that dreary garage in Fall's End when I notice a distinctive blue Suzuki parked on the forecourt. Surely that's the car Meg's bought? I recognise it from the picture she showed me on her phone. I pull up, get out, and ask a rather greasy-looking individual where the lady who bought the Suzuki might be. He frowns and I say, rather haughtily, that I'm her *friend* and he points towards the lane by the church.

'Went off that way. Said she was going for a walk. In the rain!' By his deep-throated chuckle I expect he thinks that's rather ridiculous. So do I, actually, and I head back to the car. But something makes me feel just a little uncomfortable. Meg *has* been a bit down lately. She won't say why, although I'm pretty sure it's something to do with that ghastly Barny person.

Now, I'm used to getting what I would call 'nudges' from the Good Shepherd. I tend to ignore them but am trying to learn not to, because when I get that kind of nudge, it invariably means something is afoot.

'I'm sure Meg doesn't want me interfering in her life!' I say out loud. The man in the garage is eyeing me with some amusement. I ignore him, get in the car and set off towards the Howfields.

It's been a long time. And of course, these boots are hardly sensible for trudging over fields. Flat, yes, but . . . *very* expensive. Daisy Parker really does sell the most wonderful footwear.

I soon come to the layby, and pull in behind an old Toyota.

I recognise the car.

These boots cost me a lot of money. They are now caked in mud. They're meant to be chestnut brown, but the soggy spring fields have added their own mucky colour to the beautiful, supple leather. The first leaves of spring are unfurling. *Yes, very nice. But I hope my boots aren't ruined!* I groan as I battle my way through bushes and get thwacked in the face by a rogue branch. A word the vicar would be shocked to hear drips from my glossy lips.

And then I see it. The lake that is so familiar, and yet so foreign to me now. They say never go back, don't they? Things are never the same when you do. Funny to think the lake used to be part of my summers when I was young. Mum and Dad were both alive the last time I was here.

There's a figure on the bridge. The sky is an ominous grey, I'm trying to navigate holding my umbrella while fighting through the undergrowth, and my mood is less than kind. Really! Why do I get myself into these scrapes? I should be at home, with my recipe for sausage casserole, not dragging myself through the mud like the SAS on manoeuvres!

'Paula!' My voice sounds harsh and brittle. I try to soften it, feeling my face stinging from the face-full of old twig. I stumble inelegantly onto the stone bridge. 'Paula!'

She's startled, and turns round. A resigned expression crosses her face. I get closer, and notice that hard lines are already showing from her nose to her mouth. Too young to look so careworn.

'Paula, my dear!' I say through gritted teeth, and realise my lovely soft leather gloves have something grotty on them from the bushes I've just struggled to get through. The rain patters on my umbrella. 'What on earth are you doing here? Your mother's worried sick.'

'Well,' she says, coldly, 'I'm sure the doctor can sort that out. She has to see him later.'

It appears I've been chasing after a woman who seems perfectly OK and is probably just taking some time off from her overcontrolling parent!

She leans on the stone parapet.

'Er – I wouldn't . . . not safe,' I murmur.

She glances over her shoulder, looking moody, with her dark hair, moving in the sharp breeze, too stark against her pale face. 'I am *so* done with everything. Done with my mother, done with that horrible antiques shop, all of it. I want out.'

I swallow, and gaze into the water I know is deep.

'I just wish I had a shedload of money! I'd clear off to Norfolk or Wales or somewhere. Start a new life.' She stands back from the parapet. I feel a stab of relief. I'm also wondering why she'd choose such disparate bolt-holes.

She faces me full-on, and for a moment, I'm rather afraid of her. There's a wild look in her dark eyes. *She's unstable. She's going to throw me off the bridge. Can I still swim? It's been years . . . My boots! My cashmere top! My—*

'My dad left when I was twelve. Did you know that?' Her voice is fierce. 'They were never happy. There were all these long silences . . . coldness and indifference.' She falters a bit, then continues. 'It was a Saturday morning, early. I saw him shoving suitcases in the car. I went and asked him what he was doing. He looked scared, told me to be a good girl, and that's the last I saw of him.' She swallows. 'My mother said good riddance, he was a bad man, a womaniser, then she panicked about money, and we got that depressing shop. She said I was her rock, her support. I felt too guilty to leave her. Every time I said I wanted to move out, she'd get ill! I managed to get a part-time job in the library – she didn't much like that. Then I met this man, and I'd see him down here, on the bridge.' Suddenly, there are tears in her eyes. 'I thought he was separated from his wife, but he wasn't. My mother found out and went and told her about me and him. You know what? He denied everything!'

Perhaps your interfering mother actually did you a favour! I don't say it.

'I was destroyed. I couldn't work for ages. I really loved him.' She wipes her face on her sleeve, and it's a while till she speaks again. When she does, her voice is croaky. 'And now Barny's said he isn't interested in me.'

I take a deep breath. 'Well, Paula, truthfully, I think you've had a lucky escape there.'

'He *flirted* with me!'

'To be honest, he flirts with any . . .' I stop talking, but she's ignoring me anyway.

'I went on a date for the first time in years! Then he casually tells me he doesn't *fancy* me.'

Honestly, how brutal! No finesse at all! And he's hurt Meg. Probably because he went off with Paula – or someone else. Who knows!

'Look, Paula, my dear . . .' I'm trying to sound caring although I can feel my gorgeous boots are leaking and my feet are getting wet. 'He's not the sort you want, is he, really? You're an intelligent girl. I'm sure there'll be other young men . . .' *Well, there might be if you cheered up a bit!*

'My mum will get ill on first sight of them and that'll be that.'

'Have you tried online dating?' I try, valiantly.

She eyes me as if there's something wrong with me. I shiver, holding my umbrella tightly. *If she comes at me, I can whack her . . .*

'You haven't got a clue! Look, I know you go to church. Love and goodness and all that stuff! But you know what?' She stares at me with a hint of aggression. 'I don't believe in love!'

I offer up a quick prayer. *Stand your ground, Rosemary Victoria!* 'I'm sorry you feel like that.' My voice is firm and that surprises me. 'But there *is* Someone who loves us. Better than any man could.' *Although my Arthur is such a blessing.* I see that more now than I ever did!

'God, you mean?' She laughs a mirthless laugh. 'Ha! My mother's not religious. She does her star signs and all that but she's not into church at all. Maybe that's just about enough to get me converted!'

It starts to rain harder.

I suddenly feel very fed up. 'Just get under the umbrella, will you?' I say, shortly. 'Or stand in the rain. Do what you want. I'm going home.'

'I never said I was going to the lake.' Meg is dishing up a huge portion of lasagne.

'The man at the garage said you did.'

'No, I said I was going for some milk.'

It's Thursday afternoon, the first time I've had a proper chance to talk to Meg since the events at the bridge. Another crisis with her aunt and her partner and his niece who has 'gone off the rails' has meant that she's been too preoccupied and busy to listen to anything other than my briefly telling her that Paula Bellwood was 'OK' when she appeared (late) at my little Tuesday group.

She pops the plate full of lasagne down in front of one of the customers, wipes her hands on her apron, and lowers her voice.

'So, she really is alright, then?'

'I have no idea. I haven't seen her since Tuesday. I escorted her to her car and she got in and apparently went home because I saw it later outside the shop.' I shake my head. 'I need a holiday.' *And Arthur is booking it at this very moment.* I'm going away for my sixtieth, after Easter. Oh yes. I need a break. All this doing good is exhausting. At least the make-up covers the red mark – *that blasted branch* . . .

'That lasagne looks great,' Meg's saying. 'Flora's recipe is amazing. I quite fancy some.'

Fancy . . .

'I know you like that Barny person,' I say, pouring a cup of hot chocolate for a very stout lady who is sitting on one of the rickety chairs by the window. 'But he hasn't helped Paula.' I squirt vegan cream on the top of the chocolate – a rather pointless nod, in my opinion, at calorie control – and wonder if I should say anything further. *Go for it, Rosemary!* 'I'm sorry to have to tell you, but I think he's been messing around with her and – er – let her down.'

'Eh?' She's distracted. She seems to be thinking more about the lasagne than Barny and his love life. 'Oh, I heard they were in the pub recently. Wouldn't have thought she's his type. But I suppose any port in a storm!'

That's a bit harsh! I thought she liked Barny? Perhaps she's putting on a brave face. I haven't really thought about it before, but Meg can be rather hard. I suddenly feel tiredness washing over me.

'Meg, I've done a lot of extra hours lately. Do you mind if I leave early?'

She glances at the clock over the door. 'Of course. Go now, I can manage. And thank you so much for all your help! Are you OK, though?'

I can't find any words. I just want to go home.

I know I need to go and visit Paula, really, or message Ally and ask her if she'd like to come to supper soon. *Not today!* I walk determinedly along the road, heading for my nice, safe bungalow.

'Hello, Floss!'

Archie Gainsford, waving at me from the other side of the road! A bit of kindness and this scruffy man, with his dog on a bit of thin rope, is calling me by that embarrassing old nickname – the one the kids used to taunt me with: *Flossie, Flossie, silly hair* . . . I remember the teasing, the tears, loss of appetite, sleepless nights . . . it's amazing what a good hairdresser can do with untameable locks. But here he is, yelling it across the street for all to hear. I pretend I haven't seen him, and scurry home.

Arthur is out, in Fairleigh, booking our holiday in Cornwall and buying something for his beloved garden. I barricade myself in, plonking my backside down at the kitchen table and drinking in the rather nice surroundings. I do love my kitchen. Terracotta walls, fruit-adorned tiles, oranges and lemons.

I get up at last and make myself a pot of proper coffee. I breathe in the rich aroma. Sinking down on the sofa in the sitting room, I feel relieved. *Normality.*

I drift off to sleep (I *never* sleep during the day!), but I'm woken up by a knock on the door. *Use the bell!* I get up, sincerely hoping it isn't the Jehovah's Witnesses. I am really not in the mood to have lengthy arguments about the end of the world. I am so tired I forget to use the little spyhole Arthur so thoughtfully put there. My face must register dismay as I see who's calling.

Paula hands me some cellophane-wrapped flowers. I take the fairly lifeless bouquet and stare into her sad eyes. I really, *really* don't want to invite her in.

'Just to say thanks. I'm sorry I moaned at you. It was nice of you to come and find me, nice that you care. Just wanted to say that. I can't stop,' she says, moving down the driveway. I try to look sorry. 'Got to get home. She'll worry if I'm out too long.'

I suddenly feel two things. A rush of true sympathy for this girl – life has dealt her such a difficult hand – and an intense irritation for Barny Baines. *Why couldn't he have been nicer when he told her he didn't want her?* Another bout of irritation as I think of Maureen's controlling selfishness.

When Arthur comes in later, and we're having supper – katsu chicken curry, very nice – he tells me I look exhausted, and takes my hand across the kitchen table.

'You know you can't fix people, don't you, Rosey?' he says, his kind face creasing into a smile. 'I wish you'd stop trying.'

'You're right, and I'm officially stopping. I'll enjoy Easter and our holiday then I might feel like doing good in the summer.' I get up and clear the plates. 'I'll see the vicar and tell him.'

Turns out Jason isn't free for ages. It's the middle of the following week before I can get an audience with our beloved reverend. I've taken some days off sick from the café. Meg's worried but I told her I just need a break. I manage church on Palm Sunday, and stagger through the reading; but it's all just a bit too much, and I go home before the end of the service. I cancel my little group on Tuesday. *I've had it for now.*

I head for the vicarage on Wednesday afternoon, armed with fierce intentions. I've managed to avoid most people this week. My mobile's switched off and Arthur has fielded messages on the home phone. I have just hidden away. I want my space.

Arthur's taken the car and gone off with old Alec, taking him to some hospital appointment, so I race past the café with only a brief glance at the village green, which looks so wonderful at this time of year – the big pond, with its quacking, excitable ducks, and the circular seat around the big tree, which looks so inviting. The horse chestnut, with its sweet, creamy candles, looks delicious and reminds me of days gone by. Days when I was called 'Floss' by the village boys, and hated it, and it started with Archie Gainsford . . . A long time ago.

I'm nearly sixty. I wonder if all this pastoral work has just been something to distract me from a looming big birthday.

I have to stop; I'm out of breath. I must cut down on the chocolate, and the lemon drizzle cake I'm so fond of. It's starting to rain, so I put my umbrella up and start off again towards the hill. The vicarage is opposite the church; that great sturdy building that overlooks and oversees our lives.

'Oops! I'm sorry!' I raise the umbrella and see who it is I've bumped into.

'Hello, Floss.'

Doesn't this man ever work? He looks scruffier than ever in the rain, with his old waxed jacket, flat cap and grubby trousers; his hands are shoved into the pockets. *He's just loitering around the village; why doesn't he do what he's paid for? He's a gamekeeper, isn't he? They always said he was lazy at school . . .*

'Lost me dog,' he says, glumly.

I notice he doesn't have the old animal on the rope lead by his side.

My tone is brusque. 'I hope you find it soon.'

'No, I mean she died.' His tone is laden with gloom. The rain splatters onto my brolly. He looks like he's going to cry, and doesn't say anything more. He walks away, abruptly.

I watch him, speechless. That dog wasn't just a dog, was it? It was his family, his world.

I walk round to the vicarage, marching up the sweeping gravel driveway to the beautiful Georgian building with square-paned windows and a front door that has pillars either side; I have always so admired that, but today, as I ring the bell, I feel completely disengaged.

My dear friend, Flora Fletcher, opens the door and beams at me. The beam soon fades as she observes my countenance.

'Whatever's happened?'

'I am a terrible person,' I inform her, handing her my very expensive waterproof coat, and umbrella.

'What have you done? Murdered someone?'

'Archie Gainsford's dog died.'

She starts, my wet clothes over her arm and dripping on the tiled floor.

'No, it wasn't me!' I unzip my boots. 'It's just died. And I wasn't any use at all when he was clearly upset . . . You know these boots are ruined? Where's the vicar?'

She nods towards the sitting room, silently. I walk in, feeling as if I am pushing my way through treacle. *What is wrong with me? Is this what it feels like to be weary when we're doing good, or whatever it says in the Good Book?*

The vicar is in the sitting room, just finishing a phone call, pacing around.

'Rosemary!' I'm not sure he's relieved to see me or agitated by my presence. Perhaps both? 'Can we cut this a bit short? I have to see someone. Pastoral care visit in about ten minutes . . .'

I sit down on his faded, battered old sofa, feeling a rising annoyance. Whatever the problem, I have one too. Part of which is how I am ever going to get out of this low-slung couch. My sitting down kind of forces him to sit, as well. He does, reluctantly, perching on the edge of his seat. 'What can I do for you?' He looks a bit nervous. Maybe he can sense all is not well with my soul.

'People! They're all too much . . . look, Paula's been messed about by that *dreadful* Barny Baines! He's led her on and then rejected her. And he's hurt Meg!'

'Meg?' He looks me directly in the eyes.

'Vicar, people are just too complex for me! I'm *tired*. I want to st—'

'I'm sorry you're tired. But Barny – well, it could have been worse, couldn't it? I mean . . . he could have used Paula, and I don't think he did. And Meg – well, I think she can . . . handle things.' He seems to falter at that point.

'Well, can't you at least do something about Maureen Bellwood?' I ask, plaintively. 'Oh, I realise she's frightened of being alone and all that, but honestly . . . she's so controlling!'

'I know she's overprotective,' he says, quietly.

'*Overprotective*? She's going the right way about—' I take a deep breath. 'I'm worried about Paula. She's a bright girl, but messed up. She's got *big* problems and I'm not a counsellor.'

He's silent. I suppose he's communing with the Good Shepherd. It's then that I notice he looks pallid. I sigh. I don't suppose there will be tea and toast at the vicarage today. Why am I here, anyway? Just to complain to this poor, overworked vicar about how people have got me down? How I find the more you get to know them, the more complicated it gets and the more helpless you feel? And how I am so scared of being sixty? More years behind me than I can look forward to. And what *am* I looking forward to? Old age, ill health, losing Arthur . . . oh, how I wish we could have had children! But there are no grandchildren to enjoy, no weddings, no christenings, no landmark family celebrations . . . like special birthdays . . .

'Look, Rosemary, I wonder, could you come on this pastoral visit with me? It might be appropriate, actually. One of those well-timed God things.'

'What?' I feel so drained, so totally unspiritual.

'Come on,' he says, getting up. 'Let's go and see Ally.'

I haven't been to Ally's house in years. Been to the farm shop, of course; Mr Moseley's wonderful pork products draw me here – but today what's bringing me is the pastor's white Ford and good heavens, he drives much more recklessly than Arthur does! I'm holding onto the door handle as he swerves up the drive past the shop and almost skids to a halt in the car park alongside Ally's Mini and a Range Rover. I wonder if I should ask him if he has a death wish, but it doesn't seem appropriate.

I take a few moments to recover. It's a breathtaking view, over the fields; I hear a skylark as I get out of the car. They only sing when they rise up. *My song is silent. How I need to rise up!* The rain has stopped. The meadows are smothered in bright buttercups. Horses graze the spring grass in a nearby paddock; it's all so tranquil.

I'm not sure how I feel about going into the farmhouse, that beautiful, warm red-brick building where my dear friend Lizzy lived after she got married. I was here a lot in the old days. *The past, again.* But the vicar, obviously on a mission, is striding towards the stable block. Ally lives in a self-contained flat in the main house, out of the way of her stepmother, Bella, and it's a big enough property for them never to have to meet; they never did get along. But I wonder why we have to see Ally in the stables!

Jason clearly knows his way around. I try not to step in any horse muck. There's a pile of poo and straw in the corner of the yard, and the pong of horse is making my eyes water. I know I can't hold my nose, it just wouldn't give the right impression.

We head for some new loose boxes, very smart, and Jason knocks on the end door. We go in; it's a little office, nicely painted, with a good-sized desk. Ally is sitting at it, and looks up as we enter. Her face is as miserable as Paula Bellwood's. I very nearly turn round and leave.

She's playing with a pen, twisting it in her fingers. 'Hello, Jason,' she says, dully. 'I see you've brought a friend.'

'You don't mind Rosemary being here, do you?' Jason sits down on a hard-backed seat opposite the desk, which leaves an ancient rocking chair for me. How am I meant to help the vicar on a pastoral visit when I can't even keep this blessed chair still? It was a hard enough job getting out of that sofa: *note to self, don't sit on that again!* I shudder as I remember the indignity of being hauled out of the seat by the vicar.

'I've spent the whole of my life judging people.' I notice Ally's eyes are listless. She's still twiddling the pen. 'Including *him*.'

'Who?' I really am at a loss to know what's happened.

'Archie Gainsford.'

'Oh, his dog's died. Vicar, the dog's dead . . .'

Jason shoots me a look that both tells me he knows, and that I should let Ally speak. By the end of it, hard-faced Ally has a tear trickling down her porcelain cheek, and I have a lump in my throat.

I can see the scene she paints so well. Walking into her father's study, furious because she'd found a fox had killed some young pheasants. Where was Archie? Hopeless man! Get rid of him! Why do you let him stay? He never does a decent day's work! What do you mean, he's got time off? Why? Because his *dog* died? Sack him! Get him out of that tied cottage, get someone in who'll do the job properly!

And then her father tells her, quietly. Tells her why he's always been so kind to Archie.

My lovely friend Lizzy. Died in that car crash, so many years ago. A rainy night. She missed a turning, went straight into a tree. It was Archie who found her. He rang the emergency services. He sat with her as she died.

Archie 'didn't want no fuss'. So Ally never knew. And neither did I.

I clamber out of the rocking chair (not easy – but at least the vicar doesn't have to grab me) and put my arms around Ally as she starts to sob. I look round, and see Jason, head bowed, praying. Eventually, the crying eases. I say she can come and stay with me for a while; she thanks me but says no. She needs to go and see her father; apologise for running out of the room when he told her. She doesn't even know why she did that. She's just glad that Bella is away. Maybe it'll give her a chance to talk to her father properly.

She says she feels guilty – the way she's treated Archie over the years. And me? I'm aghast at myself. *How judgemental I am!* I don't know anyone's story. Not really. Not deep down. How could I?

How do I know anyone's secrets, kept locked up in the silence of a heart?

Thursday's Maundy Service isn't particularly well attended, probably because it's such a rainy night, and everyone tends to bowl over to Fall's End because the United Reformed Church does a very good Maundy evening, with the minister washing people's feet. As he is jaw-droppingly attractive and used to be a male model, I wonder if the novelty of that is part of the draw.

According to the forecast, the rain is going to clear up tomorrow. Just as well – we have an Easter Passion Play to attend! Still, I groan, just a little. *More walking. About a mile and a half, maybe two . . . !* All puddles and budding hedgerows . . . My wonderful boots definitely leak since I had to charge about in the mud. *You know what? They weren't that comfortable. They looked good, but they pinched!* I determine to dig out my old, cheap, comfortable ones from the back of my lovely, white wood walk-in wardrobe.

I'm sitting on one of the little plastic seats at the front of the church, organised in a circle. Old Mrs Fordham is there, Jason, of course, and Meg, and surprisingly, Archie, who I've never seen in church before. He's wearing what is probably his best jumper, big and baggy but clean; he's gaunt, sitting quietly, keeping his eyes fixed on the flagstones. There are others from the congregation, and I see two of them exchanging glances as they spot Archie. *I wish they knew what I know*. But they don't. So they judge.

No sign of Paula, although I have messaged her and asked her if she'd like to come. Daisy Parker is away on 'business'. When she comes along to my Tuesday group, she does ask questions about faith – although Flora has observed, dryly, that she thinks Daisy's often amusing queries are designed to irritate and don't come from a place of genuine interest. I don't know; Daisy seems to enjoy the company. Talking of company, she *definitely* seems more interested in gentlemen friends than in any kind of religion . . . Am I just being naïve? I sigh. My attempts to encourage a genuine interest in the Good Shepherd seem so often to fall on deaf ears.

It's strange that on occasions like this, you tend to think of who *isn't* there rather than who is.

Just as we're about to begin, footsteps sound on the flagstones, and I'm surprised to see Barny Baines rather uncomfortably placing himself on the only spare chair – beside me. I notice he doesn't look at Meg, and I find myself wondering why he's even here. But I try to stop myself from judging; I've done too much of that.

More footsteps. Raising my eyes I take a deep breath. Ally walks in – with her father, Jeremy Thompson-Tracey! How well I remember him from the past. So uptight, so public school, so very proper. When he met and married Lizzy he relaxed probably for the first time in his life. Then she was gone, and Bella was there. I wonder how truly happy he's been since. He's still quite ruggedly handsome, but grief has etched deep crags into his face.

The vicar pulls another couple of chairs into the circle. This means Barny has to sit closer to me, and I catch a whiff of his rather spicy aftershave.

The door opens again. I look up with expectancy. Paula? No . . . it would be wonderful to see Arthur to walk in, but he never comes to church and I've given up asking him. He says he's kind to people, and that's his faith. I tell him good works don't make you right with God – how could they? How many times have I tried to explain that only the Good Lord's mercy and grace can do that? More deaf ears. It strikes me how many people are deaf when it comes to God and faith.

The newcomer is Flora, apologising for being late.

It's curious to see how people react when Jason says we're going to do something different this evening. I haven't been to a Maundy Service in years, remembering the Last Supper, the night Jesus was betrayed by a friend. My heart sinks when I notice the churchwarden and the lay minister standing by with jugs of water and cloths.

'We're going to pour water . . .' Jason smiles round at us as he takes one of the jugs.

Oh no! Although I have just had a pedicure . . .

'On each other's hands.'

Jason settles himself next to Meg. Turning to her, he gently suggests she cups her hands, and the water flips down over her fingers. Her eyes are closed. He uses the cloth to gently wipe them. I notice her expression – almost painful; she's affected. I am glad her faith is becoming so real to her.

Meg seems to recover herself; she pours water over Ally's outstretched hands. I study Ally's face, even though we are meant to be in prayer. Difficult to read, but I suspect it's a humbling experience for both of them. Then Ally turns to her father, and I wonder at the symbolism of the daughter serving the father in this way; I suspect years of hardness towards him may be softening. He never was one to talk about his feelings, and marrying Bella so quickly after Lizzy died didn't help the relationship with his grieving daughter. I hope there's healing tonight.

Then Jeremy Thompson-Tracey, the richest man in the village, pours water over the hands of the dejected man beside him. I notice Jeremy's brief squeeze of Archie's fingers; no response from the gamekeeper, but he takes the jug and sloshes some water clumsily, and with some embarrassment, over part of the floor as well as Flora's hands. She does the same to me, with more delicacy.

I turn to the man beside me. Barny puts his hands together, and I tip some of the warm water over them into the bowl. I dab his fingers dry. His eyes are squeezed shut. Despite my misgivings about this person, I have to admire his rather chiselled profile. Then, surprisingly, my heart just suddenly breaks for him. Why? I don't know. But as I glance around at the watching faces, I realise that it's not my heart but the Good Shepherd's that is breaking for forlorn Archie, Ally, Jeremy, even the Bellwoods . . .

I can't give up on any of them.

They're my family.

We're waiting for the rain to ease, and it does; the moon appears behind scudding clouds, revealing a starlit night. People begin to move off, quietly, the intimacy of the service binding us even as we separate and go to our homes. I see Meg loitering at the lychgate, waiting for me, but I'm hanging back. Barny's in the porch, fiddling with the collar of his jacket; he seems distracted, but something has come to me and it won't go away. I need to say it.

I walk up to him, steadily, and put a hand on his arm. He seems momentarily alarmed.

'Go and see your father, Barny. Tell him that you love him.'

He visibly relaxes, and stares at me out of empty eyes.

'Don't leave it too late,' I say, quietly.

Jason has come out of the church, and he smiles at me.

Time to go home.

PART FOUR

Jason's Story

Acceptance

This Passion Play has taken a lot of organising. I'm just glad Kathy is so enthusiastic, because frankly, I'm rather at a loss.

I'm not great at organising people. And this play is more of a Hollywood production than just a local witness of faith. Lots of people come every year, because it's quite a well-known event. It's been great to see members of my 'flock' so involved, the growing excitement, discussing the weather, talking about costumes – old Alec wanted to be a Roman centurion, and Flora Fletcher's been sorting him out, pins in her mouth while he stood rather helplessly in my sitting room, the most elderly warrior I've ever seen. I'm slightly worried about the deranged look he gets in his eyes as he wields his sword. We've insisted he doesn't walk from Fall's End to Nun's Drift or there'll be a paramedic presence that is certainly not biblical.

Anyway, they're all pulling together as a team.

And now, it's another Good Friday. I'm just recovering from a virus, and my throat's a bit dry, so I decide to get a drink before I do anything else. I go downstairs, yawning, and nearly trip over the cat, which has taken to lying across the bottom stair. I have begun to think it's on a mission to ruin my life.

I'm scratching my belly as I yawn again and slop into the kitchen. Then I realise Flora, who 'does some chores' for me, is putting the kettle on. I pull my dressing gown tight around my ancient pyjamas and we stare at each other for a moment.

'Er – wasn't expecting you today,' I mumble, just as two pieces of bread pop out of the toaster. Her expression says, *Well, clearly, Vicar!* But she tells me, 'I thought you'd appreciate a good breakfast!' while grabbing the toast, turning to the hob and ladling scrambled eggs onto a plate.

'I'll get dressed,' I mutter, but she slaps the food down on the table without ceremony.

'It's going to be a wonderful day,' she says, pouring me a cup of tea. 'My friend Alec is so looking forward to being a soldier. Good job that sword's plastic.'

She starts talking about how Alec is really into Star Wars, but I don't want to pursue that conversation. I eat my eggs and drink my tea. My phone is bleeping away with WhatsApp messages. I check them. Arthur's at the church already, with the churchwarden, manoeuvring the 'stone' that Barny made out of I-don't-know-what in front of the porch. After the dramatic rolling away of the stone, the parishioners and whoever else will enter into St Saviour's for a Good Friday service. A great idea – Kathy's

– but I wonder what it says about our church being likened to a tomb!

Flora's clearly excited about the Passion Play, pageant, or whatever they're labelling it. She says it brings the good news alive, it always draws a crowd, and did I know the *Fairleigh Gazette* will be there? I feel like saying 'so what' as I remember the last time we did this play. I'd only just arrived in Nun's Drift, and a lot of people were getting rained on and trying to be bright although everything was damp. Anyway, I make no comment. As I gaze out of the large, square-paned window into the vicarage garden, I can see it's sunny, with fluffy, flat-bottomed Suffolk clouds drifting across the sky, the breeze making the blossom flutter across the lawn like confetti.

'Barny needs to cut that grass as soon as it's dry,' remarks Flora.

Barny! He told me he's going to see his father today. Such a good idea! Good for Rosemary, suggesting it! I pray he'll repair bridges, get some peace, build up some sort of relationship with his dad, even at this late stage. He'll be out of his comfort zone, but . . .

Flora pours me another cup of tea. I'm remembering Rosemary's words to me, the exhaustion of pastoral care so evident in her face. I need to talk with her about boundaries. About triggers. About walking alongside as a servant, not trying to fix people.

I yawn, this time with my hand over my mouth. I've got next week off. I'm going to spend some time at a retreat house with my mentor, Rev Mark from the Howfields. Need to think about promises made. My future.

'I'm sorry I couldn't do bacon this morning.'

'I'm fine, Flora, really. The eggs were great.'

'You'd have got the bacon, but – that blasted cat. Oh, sorry, Vicar. But you know what happened.'

Yes, I remember, and shudder. *Another* incident concerning the cat. I wonder if I can find a new home for it after Easter.

'Anyway, you want something more than toast and marmalade or that rubbishy muesli you like when you've got walking to do. You've only just got over that virus.'

'Thank you for your concern,' I say, with a smile. 'It's appreciated.'

'Huh!' She snatches my empty plate off the table.

'You don't know anyone who wants a feline friend, do you?' I ask, as she starts washing up.

She glances over her shoulder. *Hmm. That's an answer, right there.*

I'm observing my study, nearly finished, nearly ready to inhabit again. I've missed it. It just isn't the same, working in my sitting room. I lean against the doorframe. The cat didn't cause such devastation that I needed to totally redecorate, but a new carpet was certainly necessary. That's when I thought about the wallpaper and how old it all was. Barny's a great decorator – and he's made a good start . . .

Anxiety washes over me all of a sudden. No! I can't give in to this. The confusion. The doubt. The lack of being able to connect with God. I can pray for others, but I can't pray for myself. I used to be so certain. And now – what a hypocrite I am! If anyone knew . . .

I take the stairs two at a time, dress quickly, and head for the front door. I need some fresh air. Yes, I'll get plenty of that later, but for now, before everything begins – I need to be alone.

I can't go to the church. I can already see people hanging around outside; getting everything ready for later.

I walk down the hill into the village, over the green, noticing the swathe of daffodils by the pond, and the scruffy pub sign that really needs replacing. I keep my head down, and find the narrow footpath beside the Half Moon. *Please, I don't want to meet anybody.*

This path runs alongside some allotments, leading to a grassy space where there's an oak tree that I like to sit under during the summer months. It's a popular place for dogwalkers, but this morning it seems that the whole village has decided to take their canine companions for an early morning stroll. The dogs are barking and chasing each other. A spaniel bowls into me, then a golden retriever rushes up and licks my hand. Several people see me, and call out.

'Hello, Vicar! Looking forward to the pageant? We're all going. Me and my family.'

'Better weather this year, Vicar! It's gonna be great.'

'You seen old Alec dressed up as a soldier? He's wandering round the village, waving his sword about.'

'We'll all be there, Vicar! See you later!'

I smile and wave.

Then I turn on my heel and head back to the vicarage.

Rev Kathy is busy. She's instructing the young man who's playing Jesus on how to carry the cross ('It's not that big – a great strapping lad like you, don't be such a wimp!') and he's saying he's hoping it won't affect his leg because last year he pulled his adductor muscle.

'We've practised this, Jack!' she points out, stoically. 'You'll be fine!'

'Alright, alright.' He scratches his beard, grown especially for the occasion, as he keeps telling us all.

The sun's still shining. People are already gathering in the market square to watch the spectacle. There's a round of applause when the Roman centurions turn up. Someone wolf whistles. Jack adjusts his long white robe and glares at his sniggering mates, huddled by the charity shop, as he picks up the fairly large wooden cross.

'That's a less than godly glare!' observes Kathy, and I laugh.

'Great turnout.' I nod towards the people of Fall's End and elsewhere, little knots staring at the players.

The beefy blokes dressed as Roman centurions look very good; a bit more believable than Alec's attempt, but rather ruined by the fact that one of them is on his phone, explaining – firmly, and with quite a few expletives – that he doesn't want 'vegetarian muck' for dinner but wants pie and mash, and if he has to eat any more falafel, he'll move out. The other is a local farmhand who greets me with a cheery, 'Alright, Vicar?' before giving his girlfriend a kiss.

The 'disciples' are made up from both congregations. Someone tells me that the man who sells cheese at Fall's End market is playing the part of Simon Peter, but I've rarely been to that market and I don't know him. Arthur is with Rosemary. I wonder if he'll manage the mile and a half to our village. But he seems pretty fit, chatting away to a couple of the old boys I recognise from the local gardening club. *Look, he's involved in something churchy, it's got to be good.*

Meg is Mary Magdalene, and is adjusting a fairly ill-fitting long dress, with her chestnut hair refusing to be totally constrained under the hooded part of the costume. I think she looks wonderful. I can hardly tear my eyes from her.

Then I spot Paula Bellwood in the crowd. Apparently, Rosemary messaged her last night and asked her to do something useful, so she's handing out leaflets informing people of the timing of everything. She doesn't look happy, but then, she never does.

Ally is hanging around, smoothing her ponytail, staring into space; her dad isn't with her. He's gone to pick up Bella from the station. I find it interesting that he came to church last evening; will he come again, when Bella's around? Her lack of interest in God is well known in the village. I remember the Maundy Service; Jeremy looking awkward, as ever, but smiling politely at people who very nearly curtsied or doffed their caps. Well, he is landed gentry, I suppose. When he poured water on Archie's hands, I nearly wept with the poignancy, and I suspect I wasn't the only one.

I notice Archie hovering around at the edge of the crowd, looking lost. I really must speak to him later.

A sudden gust of wind whips my hair and we set off, following Jack. It's a very pleasant walk along the road to the village I have grown to love. There's a great view of the woods on the Thompson-Tracey estate, the trees bursting with new life. A perfect setting for an Easter pageant.

Someone is walking beside me; a woman. It's Ally, and I feel a slight disappointment that it's not Meg. But I determine to shelve those feelings today. I must. I have to get a grip. I'll review them on retreat, not now. I look round. Meg's walking with Rosemary, deep in conversation. Paula is alongside Arthur, listening as he chatters to her, animatedly.

'I've never done this walk before. Not sure what the point is, really,' says Ally.

'It's remembering.'

'Oh, right.' She seems unimpressed. 'I think that chap playing Jesus is dating Daisy Parker. He looks tough but he's struggling a bit.' She smirks. 'Maybe you'll need to carry the cross.'

'Believe me,' I say, wearily, 'at times I feel I already do.'

'Well organised, though,' she comments.

'It's Kathy's bag, really. I think it's her *raison d'être*.'

'Well, we all need one, I suppose.' She wrinkles her retrousse nose. 'I really don't like Fall's End. It's so downmarket.'

Has she said that to deliberately goad me?

'Ah,' I reply, 'but this road leads to something better.'

Now, she laughs. 'OK, you're spiritualising.'

'Yeah, that's kind of what I do.'

'I was talking to Meg,' she says, with a sideways glance. 'She's been on about that bridge on our land – the one they say is haunted. Crosses the lake. She loves it. It's on the edge of those woods.' She points. 'Ever been there?'

'No.' *Is that the bridge Barny was talking about?*

'You scared of ghosts?'

'I'm scared of a lot of things, Ally, but not ghosts,' I say, fervently. 'It's the living that worry me more than anything hanging around calling itself a ghost.'

'Yeah.' She pushes her hands deep into her gilet pockets. 'We're a weird bunch, humans, aren't we? We think we know everything, and you know what? We don't know a thing, really, do we?'

I'm surprised to hear her speaking like that, but maybe in the light of recent events, she's got good reason to think more deeply about life, about humanity, about everything.

'Well, not much, I suppose. Always learning. The more I go on, the less I know. Anyway, this bridge. What's so special about it?'

'I don't know. Haven't been down there for ages. Peaceful, I guess. Undisturbed.'

Hmm, is it?

'Uh-oh!' she stops, suddenly.

Jack is putting the cross down, rubbing his leg.

'Oh no!' groans Kathy, as she steps forward.

'I'm OK!' says Jack, bravely.

'Don't worry, mate.' I watch as Archie approaches him – and grips the cross. 'I'll help you, alright?'

I suddenly feel very touched, and I wonder if my companion is now tight-lipped because she's holding back tears. She mumbles something, and falls back into the crowd. I carry on walking.

There's some heavy breathing at my right hand, and Rosemary's there. I glance over my shoulder and see Meg talking to Paula. *Meg is so good with people. She would make such an excellent . . .*

'Good turnout!' Rosemary is panting, her mascara slightly smudged with the effort of walking – she needs to lose a few pounds. 'Sometimes seeing things is easier than reading about them. Don't you think?'

'Yes, I do. That's why I like stained glass. Tells a story.' My eyes dart back to Meg, and I nearly trip.

'Are you alright, Vicar? You're looking a bit pasty, if you don't mind me saying so.'

I do mind, but I don't comment. *Focus, Jason!* 'How are you feeling, now, Rosemary? Glad you said what you did to Barny, by the way. He really listened.'

'Oh, I should think he'd already thought about visiting his dad and just need a prod. Good grief, I wish I'd worn different boots. These old ones – I don't know what's happened to my feet . . .' We pass a rustic gate. I feel so tempted so lean on it. 'I need some time off, I know that,' she's saying. 'But I rather think you do too. All this vicaring stuff takes its toll, doesn't it?'

I smile wanly.

We reach a bend. I love this turn in this road, where all of a sudden, we see Nun's Drift for the first time; a picture of beauty, down the hill, nestling in the valley, thatched roofs quaint and slate roofs shining in the morning sunlight.

We stop by a large detached property, which has a massive garden, with a lawn to the left and a parking area and some sheds with an orchard behind them to the right. They've set out trestle tables on the grass, with water and other cold drinks for anyone who might need sustenance. The couple that owns the house seem very relieved that it's not raining and make the same observation about the weather that everyone else has that day. I notice the dwarf tulips and cheerful narcissi growing beside the drive, nodding their heads in the gentle breeze, as if approving what we're doing; the apple trees are in full blossom, leaning over the sheds.

There's some drama, mostly around the fact that 'Simon of Cyrene' is meant to be helping Jesus with the cross for the next part of the journey, and Archie got there first. There are a few strong words that aren't in the Bible.

The re-enactment that accompanies the refreshment is meant to be staged as a brief rest for the older members of the crowd, and the infirm. So those who need it make the most of a little break.

Kathy comes alongside, puffing a little with stout walking and the sheer effort of organising such an awesome 'play'.

'Look at their faces! People who don't come to church.' She stares at the throng of people. I don't know if most of them do or don't; they could be her parishioners for all I know. 'I'm just relieved we haven't blocked the road for any tractors or whatever. That happened the year before last. Honking horns, rude language, the apostle John shouting that he'd call the cops, disaster.'

'So that's why someone suggested having a "water break" – not just out of kindness, but to prevent road rage,' I laugh.

She grins. 'You know, I just love it. Getting everyone together like this.' This fifty-something woman with no particular physical appeal chuckles, her visage brightening into something beautiful.

And then it happens.

Jack, as Jesus, turns to face me. The sun's behind him. He's holding the cross, and he's about to hand it over to the guy playing Simon of Cyrene, but he hesitates.

He's wearing a purple robe, a rough 'crown of thorns' and well-arranged make-up on his face, plus stains on his clothing to show that he's been beaten. Now, I know the 'props' have been arranged by the girl who works in the hairdressers in Nun's Drift. And I know Ian, farmer Tony's labourer, is only pretending to be the centurion who pushes 'Jesus' forward before Simon takes up the cross.

Jesus stumbles, and falls. And all of a sudden it isn't Jack. It's my Saviour, too weak with the beating to even carry the cross where he took all my rubbish and paid the price for it, exchanging my bad stuff for his good in the huge cosmic swap I can never fully understand.

There's something powerful happening.

This is what it's all about.

This, Jason.

This, this, this.

I feel shaky, and someone asks me if I'm OK. The voice seems to come from a long way off. I ask if I can use the loo. I do, and then, as I walk back through the kitchen, the lady of the house suggests I take a minute and sit down. She's a retired nurse, she says. She sits at the table, and offers me a slice of walnut cake. She says I look like I need some sugar. Maybe I do. I also know I need a rest. A rest from some tumultuous thoughts.

'I'm alright, really,' I assure her.

She doesn't look convinced. I explain I've been poorly with a virus. Then I eat the cake and glance around the enormous kitchen, with its well-appointed cupboards, Aga, sensible farmhouse table with checkered tablecloth, blue china on the windowsill and red tiles on the floor.

I remember the almost divine moment I had before I felt strange.

I rub my hand over my face.

'Jason! What happened? Someone said you were ill.'

We're outside the pub in Nun's Drift, and Meg's face is full of worry; her hand is on my arm. I move away. It's the first time we've properly spoken since that Monday, and I dismiss the concern.

'Just a bit dizzy. I've been ill, probably a bit stupid to do all this walking. Got some time off next week.'

The hooded part of her costume has come down, and is around her shoulders. I look away, at the three wooden crosses, erected on the village green; they're empty. The two thieves and Jesus are tied there no longer. The drama has been enacted. Jesus has been taken to the tomb. Or rather, Jack has disappeared into the Half Moon to get changed for his final appearance in the churchyard.

I had a ride to Nun's Drift in the nurse's 4x4. I have never been so grateful for a lift in my life. But I feel nettled when I realise elderly Arthur has completed the walk and is fighting fit, whereas me? I will probably never live this down.

'You look washed out.' I look at Meg now; her liquid green eyes are full of affection I can't return.

'I'm fine!' I put a hand up and walk towards St Saviour's.

I don't want this affection. I don't want anything.

I'm just her priest, her vicar.

Leave me alone, Meg.

Leave me alone.

I don't know how I got through it, I felt so drained, but I did.

Barny's 'stone' had been rolled away from the entrance to the church – cue old Alec, who really has missed his calling as an actor, melodramatically putting a hand to his heart and staggering about before collapsing onto a bench, which was meant to be part of the drama but someone started calling the emergency services till he opened his eyes and told them to stop being so silly. He was, after all, meant to be guarding the tomb and had just seen an angel – the girl from the Co-op, tinsel halo askew. An argument nearly ensued but fortunately Rosemary placated Alec with a promise of a nice lunch at their place.

After that, Jack had appeared in white robes with his arms outstretched and Meg as Mary Magdalene tried to touch him, just as in the Gospel story. A thought went through my head: *Mary believed he was just the gardener. Until he called her by her name.*

I squinted at Jack against the sun, but I couldn't regain the feeling I had before. He was Jack, playing Jesus (with a limp) but there was nothing special . . . Nothing like what happened earlier. What *did* happen, then?

Everyone clapped. Jack actually bowed. Kathy looked at me and rolled her eyes. I could just see her thinking, 'It's not a performance!'

No, it wasn't.

Of course, a sombre Good Friday service was never going to work. There was too much of a buzz in the packed church.

'Great play. Best one ever!' I heard it many times as I shook people's hands at the door.

'Well done, Vicar! And well done, Rev Kathy! You deserve a medal.'

'Where's Jack? He did well, didn't he?'

'Who was that old tramp who carried the cross part-way?'

Old tramp! I winced as I heard that. Looked like Archie had gone, anyway.

Local press, lots of people. Did they come for the show, or did it mean something to them?

Well, it did to me.

Now, lying on my bed, I run through that scene outside the water-break house again and again. I come to the conclusion that whatever happened must have been a touch from God. *Or your imagination. Your mind just played tricks on you, Jason.*

I'm too weary to get undressed. Kathy's been on the phone, so has Rosemary, fussing about me. *I'm fine. I just need a break.*

Meg and I WhatsApped a lot. I knew we were getting closer, and I knew it wasn't right. But I let it go on. I usually switch my phone off in the evening; but I didn't, and we were messaging till about ten most nights. Only for a while. But . . .

I told myself it was safe enough; she and Barny were friendly, and while I had to park any uneasy feelings around that, I had a feeling she wasn't 'into him'. We got on too well. And then I was in the café and our hands touched. That was it. Just an accidental thing. Electric. I felt disorientated. She felt something too, because nothing's been the same since.

She doesn't message me now. I don't message her. And she's been 'too busy' to attend my groups.

I miss the fun banter, the easy way we got along. Yes, I miss her. But I don't want to.

I wake up on Saturday morning and my heart is flipping about. I don't want to look at my phone because I'm wondering whether Meg has messaged me. How about having a rest from WhatsApp? I can't, of course. Or can I? Mark told me to get two phones. Personal and work. Why have I never done that?

OK, so today I go into Fairleigh and I buy a new phone. Personal. Only give the number out to a few people. Not Meg. Turn the work one off whenever I feel it's appropriate – only use it for pastoral calls. Then I'll at least feel a little in charge of who contacts me and when.

I really like Easter Saturday. It's a weird day, in-between the build-up to the crucifixion, the sadness of Good Friday, and the excitement Resurrection Sunday brings. Mark refuses to call it Easter Day. He wasn't around yesterday; he had an upset stomach, and I'm just hoping he'll be OK for Monday, and going away. He says it's something he ate. I remember visiting his home; his wife's sweet but she's not much of a cook; they seem to live on take-aways. *Meg's a great cook.*

Flora's hovering in the kitchen and I wonder if she's been at the vicarage all night. I'm dressed, I had a good night's sleep and I'm feeling better. But I'm not 100 per cent fit. Only tomorrow's service to get through. Welcoming the new day, the dawn, and then the business of the Easter service, which will be packed and powerful.

I drink my tea very quickly, aware of Flora watching me, silently handing me a bowl of the muesli she so despises. I can't get out of the door fast enough. I used to be like this, years ago, when anxiety was my boss. I know I can't go back to that. I have to sort myself out.

The car won't start.

You're kidding me!

No. It will not start.

'You're with the RAC, aren't you, Vicar?' asks Flora, dithering about on the front step.

I slam the car door with force.

'I suppose you could pray about it . . .' Her voice trails off as I fiercely tap the number of the RAC into my phone.

Sometime later, the cheerful vehicle recovery man informs me that I've got a flat battery. Did I leave the lights on? *Oh, Jason!* I never was good with cars. But my memory – where's my mind? How on earth could I have left the lights on, and no one spotted that? Not even . . . well, who? No houses opposite – St Saviour's looms over the road. How isolated I am!

The RAC man tells me I have to charge the battery. Flora calls Rosemary, and Arthur swiftly appears with a battery charger. Why are people so helpful?

I feel out of control. I could take the car for a drive to charge up the battery. Like, to Fairleigh, to buy a phone. Fifteen-mile round trip. I could hammer along the bypass.

I can't turn Arthur's offer of assistance down, though, so I am gracious and decide to go for a long walk instead. I have just *got* to get out, get alone, get some space.

'Vicar, you weren't well yesterday,' says Flora, pleadingly. 'Do you really think it's wise to go for a walk?'

I wave my phone at her as I push my feet into my wellies. I point out I'm taking a bag of liquorice allsorts, my favourite treat, just in case I feel a bit 'off'. She looks unconvinced and offers to make some jam sandwiches; kind, but I say no. She insists I take a bottle of water.

I start off down the driveway. *Jam sandwiches!* I haven't had them since I was a kid. I used to make them myself, my daily sandwiches. No choice, my mum was never around. She wasn't much of a mother, really. Not in the true sense. I was taking care of myself since I was – oh, I can't remember – and dodging the fists of her boyfriend, as well as avoiding his cutting remarks; words I still hear to this day. I try to put this in the past, but when I'm feeling tired or sick, it still haunts me.

'Like the undead,' I mutter to myself as I set off down the hill to the village, bathed in the rich golden glow of a new day, making Nun's Drift look as warm and welcoming as I know it is. One of the residents is messing around with a bin in his front garden and bids me a bright good morning, as if to make the point.

Haunting . . . undead. What did Ally say yesterday about ghosts? Something about that bridge at Fall's End. Might be a bit of a trek, a couple of miles, I should think. But I feel fine and I sort of know where I'm heading. Ally had pointed to the woods at the edge of the Thompson-Tracey spread. Barny and Ally both said it's peaceful. That's where I'm going. Good to have something to aim for.

I start along Stile Road. There's that great pub in Fall's End, where I determine to have lunch. As I walk, I find my breathing slows down. I pass the B&B with the wrought-iron fence, and Flora's flint cottage, noticing that Barny's van is missing – I briefly wonder how he is – the small Co-op, and then the pavement disappears and it's just hedgerows, the verge dotted with what some country people call 'shirt buttons', early stitchwort, and bluebells adorning the greenness with drops of sky. I bend down when I come to a large patch; the scent is intoxicating as the morning sun warms them.

No vehicles. Good. I take a swig of water. Low Saturday. The space between desolation and new hope. Why do we live so much in confusion when we know that Easter Sunday is just around the corner? It strikes me that I spend a lot of my life living in the 'I don't know what to make of it' disappointment of that Saturday. The turmoil, the not understanding, the hopes dashed, the promises unfulfilled. *So, what were you expecting, Jason?*

What *did* I expect when I became a priest?

Trouble? Pressure? Problems? Yes. Helping? Encouraging? Inspiring? Serving the highest cause? Yes. Total commitment, focus and straightforward service, no complications? Yes. Did I get that? No.

I remember taking that vow of celibacy.

I also remember conversations.

'Jason, that's serious. Be sure it's God.'

'Aw, Jason, that's a lonely life!'

'You might meet someone . . . what then?'

'There's nothing wrong in having a family, Jason, it's a blessing!'

'That's a massive sacrifice – no wife, no kids?'

I'd replied with certainty: 'No distractions.'

Yeah, right.

I come to the big house with the orchard and the 4x4 in the drive, alongside a brand-new BMW. Such a welcome yesterday, but today the curtains are drawn and there's no sign of life.

For some reason, I remember my gran. She was kind to me when I was young and I wanted to live with her, get away from raging eyes and fists. But she was ill; she died when I was ten. I used to stand at her gate and wish she was still there, but there was no welcome in that place anymore, just a new porch, and strangers walking down the newly paved path, glancing idly at a little boy they didn't know staring at a house that had meant so much.

Life moves on. Things change.

I realise I don't like change.

I linger by the fence, trying to accurately recall whatever it was I thought I saw when Jack stumbled in the garden.

My phone bleeps in my pocket. I switch it off. I don't care who it is, I don't want to know.

I carry on walking. Then, on the left-hand side of the road, I spot a brick-built cottage with a weathervane on the slate roof, featuring a dog. The cottage is set in the middle of a large garden, with well dug-over flowerbeds, borders ready for vegetables, and a neat lawn. Of course, it's Archie's place. As I stop and look at it, I can see it's well-maintained. Jeremy Thompson-Tracey owes Archie so much; it looks as if he's taken care of him. It suddenly comes to me: *Jason, why have you never visited Archie? You knew where he lived. All you ever do is pass by.* I'm chastened.

There's no movement in the cottage from what I can see, just a washing line to the side of the property, with a shirt flapping on it. Been out all night, I guess. They say Archie used to live here with his mum, that he always had a dog with him.

Living alone with a series of dogs for company. What sort of life was that? I wonder if he's ever had a girlfriend. He's certainly never been married. Then it hits me. *When it comes down to it, there's not much difference between you and him, really, is there, Jason? Maybe you should buy a Labrador!*

I know I should pay Archie a visit. Of course I should! Later, on the way back. *You don't know he'll be in, Jason.* I sigh. I just can't do it right now. It's no good, he'll have to wait. I need to be on my own. The argument continues in my mind as I start walking again.

It only seems like five minutes since I was here before, and of course, it isn't even twenty-four hours ago. But I'm pleased with myself when I reach the crummy garage at Fall's End, and sit on the low wall, tempted by the liquorice allsorts. I have a few and decide to leave the rest for the walk home – just in case I feel weird.

A slim, rather grimy-looking character is on the forecourt, about to wash one of the vehicles for sale. He must recognise me from yesterday because he grins.

'Mornin', Reverend. I'd have thought you'd had enough of walkin', or can't you Nun's Drift types keep away from us?'

I smile. *Now, where's this bridge? How do I get to it?*

Fortified by the liquorice allsorts, I decide to ask the garage man.

'I dunno what it is with people, wantin' to see that old bridge.' He scratches his head. 'There's nothin' there, you know. Nothin'.'

He's right, of course. There's nothing here.

I've found it, after struggling through some bushes, and to me, it's a massive disappointment. There are metalwork gates, partly open, rusting, unimpressive, not doing their job. It's easy to access the bridge.

The lake's a bit overgrown. But it is *very* large.

I walk across the stone bridge, noticing the broken bits, and wondering how safe it is. The other side has more metal gates, more dilapidated than the others, and then an ordinary, five-barred wooden one. I lean on it, gazing into an empty field beyond. Nothing there speaks of anything extraordinary. I looked online and didn't find a lot about this place; only that the bridge once led to some kind of religious house. *I so need a retreat.* It crosses my mind: Does a cloistered life seem appealing? *Running away again, Jason, just like Barny does?* Barny's been facing his demons, though, hasn't he? Or at least some of them.

I wander back along the bridge, and stand for a moment, staring out at the quiet water. OK, the sun's light glittering on the surface is nice. Seen better, seen worse. But generally, it's just an old bridge to nowhere. Disappointing.

What did I expect? Outstanding beauty? Perfection? Did I expect to encounter God? *That seems to happen in unexpected places at unexpected times . . .*

Then I have another thought, and not a spiritual one.

This place seems to have become popular with someone I really don't want to see just now. I don't want her turning up and disturbing the still waters of my world. The very thought makes anxiety well in my chest.

I get off the bridge and lean against a large ash tree.

Breathe, Jason.

I can't fight this.

Stop trying. Switch your phone on.

For a moment, I'm disorientated. I stumble over some curling tree roots as I try to find my way back to the field beyond.

Switch the phone on.

In the end, I give up and obey the insistent, nagging feeling. I'll have to switch it on soon, anyway. I look at it with loathing. It dictates my life.

Two missed phone calls – Flora and Arthur. Several messages. Nothing from Meg. I wonder where she is, who she's with. *Stop it, Jason.* One of the messages is from Jeremy Thompson-Tracey; it lifts my spirits, and I'm suddenly grateful I looked at my phone.

Another of the messages is from Barny. He's decided to stay with his dad for the whole of the Easter weekend. They've been talking. It's not easy, but something has shifted. For the first time he's been able to really listen to his dad's story, and his dad has really listened to him too. It's a start.

'Tell Rosemary', he says, 'I'm grateful for the push.'

Barny's difficult, but the wall's coming down, brick by brick . . . I suddenly wonder how he felt when I poured water on Meg's hands on Thursday. *Stupid, Jason.* I sat down next to her before I could think what I was doing. Didn't I?

My mind flicks to Rosemary. She has such a big heart; she really cares about wounded people. But damaged people can be like broken toys . . . they have a tendency to hurt others, unintentionally.

A blackbird skips past me, a long stalk of dried grass in its beak. I look up and catch sight of a hare running towards the wood. Never seen one in the flesh before; what a breathtakingly beautiful creature.

I continue my journey.

In the King's Arms, I choose a steak pie from the glossy menu, and wash it down with real ale. There are some old fellas at the bar, drinking beer, muttering about football and cricket. A couple at the table next to me seem to be having an argument about whether they can afford a new conservatory. A woman walks in complaining to her partner about the lack of parking in this village.

The fireplace is alive with a massive, roaring fire, and the smell of burning wood is comforting. I suppose they'll stop making up the fire soon, but today is still enough 'spring' rather than 'summer' to need some extra warmth. The restaurant side of the pub seems busy, but the bar is quiet. I can't believe people are leaving me alone. It's so good just to be on my own like this. I know I need to factor breaks into my day, into my life, a lot more than I do. I determine to start fresh when I'm back from retreat.

Then it strikes me. *Wait! No one is talking about the events of yesterday*. So much planning by Kathy, so much practise and hard work. Such an important, life-changing story. They're talking about football and cricket and conservatories and cars.

OK, so being left alone is good. But did all of that mean *nothing* to some people?

Well, it meant something to me! And maybe that's the point. I remember what happened when I saw 'Jesus' stumble. How I wish I could re-run that mystical moment in my mind, seeing clearly . . . it's as if it's there but elusive, I can't quite grasp the memory. I close my eyes. I see fragments. Just enough. I feel a sudden rush of joy.

I finish my ale, get up from my seat, and take one last look at the occupants of the bar. The barman, wiping a glass with a cloth, is talking to the woman and her partner about cars. The old fellas are still talking about sport. The warring couple have fallen silent and are scrolling through their phones.

I shut the door behind me and take a deep breath. *They may not listen, they may not see the point, but that doesn't mean we stop inviting them.*

As I make my way back along the road to Nun's Drift, I feel as if I've visited doubt and come away believing. It's an odd feeling. I stop by Archie's gate. I see a figure getting the shirt off the line.

Better do that visit.

'You've just got to stop fighting, Jason.'

I look at Mark, and he looks at me.

'Because that's what you're doing.' He shrugs his shoulders. 'You're in two minds.'

Flora puts a bacon roll down before each of us. The Easter sunrise service is always so stunning – well, when there *is* a sunrise and it isn't a damp day. It's great that we could do it with St Mary's and the Howfields' churches this year. But I'm shattered, and Mark says I look unwell.

When I welcomed the dawn this morning, representing the new start in life I believe our Faith gives to us, I saw it again . . . the picture of Jesus, falling to his knees under the weight of all my 'stuff', and I felt peace. But I'm in the vicarage now, and talking with Mark has brought the heaviness back. He isn't a celibate, so he doesn't understand as well as he might, but he's a great spiritual director and mentor. I've confided in him, and he suggests I talk to Father Simon at the priory near Fairleigh.

'This is inner turmoil, mate,' he says, cheerfully biting into his breakfast bap.

'You don't say.'

'Ah, you'll be OK. We'll have a great time away. Restful. Just what you need. And don't forget. Talk to Father Simon. He's a good bloke.'

'Augustinian, isn't he?' I rub my eyes.

'Yep. Had lunch there a few weeks back. All those friars chat about is football and cars.'

Hmm! Not much difference in conversation to the pub in Fall's End, then.

'There used to be some sort of priory at the edge of Nun's Drift,' I remark.

'Oh, you mean by the bridge at Fall's End? Yeah, that was Augustinian, I think. Or was it Franciscan?'

Honestly! Does *everyone* know about this place? Mark's licking tomato sauce off his fingers.

'Yeah, real spiritual hideaway from what I hear. A sort of *thin place*, you know, where heaven kind of meets earth.'

I stir my tea in silence.

'They also say it's haunted.' He chuckles. 'Funny how people react in different ways to the peace of a place. I've been there a few times. Idyllic. You should go.'

I say nothing.

He hasn't quite finished his roll, but scrapes his chair back, standing and chewing before he leaves for his own parish. 'Picking you up at ten tomorrow, remember.'

I want to go back to bed, but I have a service to take.

Bank Holiday Monday. Another fine day.

I flick on the indicator, pulling into the layby. I have an hour and a half before Mark picks me up.

Have I missed something? What is it? Why do people – even *Barny* – seem to experience something of the Divine at this lake, and I didn't?

As I start to trudge along the side of the meadow, I remember the hare I noticed racing so freely across the field. Running, rushing. Panicked beauty.

Am I going to encounter the Good Shepherd here today? Or not? And why am I bothering, considering I'm about to go on retreat anyway?

I fight through branches that are bursting with greenery. We're nearly into verdant, lush May, my favourite month.

So many branches! Why is it so hard to get to the bridge?

I'm relieved to see the gates at last. I stumble through them, onto the stone. *I bet the hare never comes here.* Too free, running in zigzags, living his life. No time to watch the water.

A few mallards swim by. One dives under the water, and surfaces, shaking the sparkling water off his back. I watch them swim away, till they're dots in the distance. I lean over the parapet, carefully. Circles in the water indicate there are fish. I watch the ripples spreading out. One fish can cause so much disturbance to the stillness; like one thought – one person.

Oh, Lord, I miss Meg's company, the friendship, the easy intimacy. But I can't do anything about it.

And then, peace descends like a sudden shower.

You're just a man, Jason. You're not God. Don't be so hard on yourself. Remember – the Good Shepherd is the perfect one. You're not.

Back in the car, I take a moment before I turn the engine on.

The bridge is fine, but I'm still not sure it's too special. Maybe it's coming with a level of expectancy, an openness, a humility, that makes the difference. There's something about getting away from the hubbub of daily life to be in silence. But it's more about being open in the heart.

I ponder, not for the first time, how we can never truly know the heart of another; we are only, in the end, accountable for our own decisions, actions and reactions.

Accept it, Jason.

I have to. This is the way it is.

I'm celibate, that's a vow; I'm also attracted to Meg, because I'm human, and she's a gorgeous woman, and I like her. But Meg won't be the only woman I meet and am attracted to throughout my life. I need to know how to deal with it. Firm boundaries . . .

Yes, I will go and talk to Father Simon.

An Ending

Meg's Story

I'm lying on my bed; Thursday evening, silent, no bell-ringers at work at St Saviour's; that's Wednesdays. Still, I'm thinking about the bells and how I used to find them annoying, but now I don't.

I love my little room, and the café; everything that should match and doesn't, shouldn't work and does. The old chairs, painted by my aunt, the misshaped pots and jars, some of which she made herself out of air-dried clay, shells gathered from seaside trips, and a wide variety of plates, cups and saucers and little jugs. I'm so lucky – no, *blessed* – to have this life. Maybe I will have adventures and add to the pots and shells, memories of happy times. I hope so.

Rain is pattering against my window. The broken pane remains unfixed; it's OK.

This place is beautiful, but it's not perfect.

I'm not perfect.

I need to get up, get changed. I'm due at Rosemary's at 7.30 p.m. Some of us have been invited for a pre-birthday buffet. She's touchy about her age so I'm surprised she's having any kind of party for what she calls a 'big birthday'. Anyway, we all offered to take her out for a meal but she's insisting we come to her place. She's off to Cornwall soon with Arthur and she so deserves a good break.

I open the wardrobe door and look at myself in the full-length mirror. I've put weight on during the past year, but it suits me. I don't like comparing myself with others, and I'm not as good-looking as Ally, but I'm not unattractive.

I'm nearly twenty-seven, and by that age, my mother was married. Of course, she divorced and married again. I wonder if I will marry at all.

I grab a dress from the wardrobe. Rosemary has shared the guest list with me, and there may be some awkward moments. Jason returned from his retreat on Sunday, but I haven't seen him. I hope he found his time away helpful. *His time away from me.* Barny's back, too. He hasn't been to see me, or called me. Can't blame him.

I like male company. I always have. But have I been as careful with hearts as I could have been? No, of course not. I rest my head against the wardrobe door. I hope I'm getting less self-centred. I did the right thing with Barny and I'm not naïve enough to think Jason is the only man I will ever be attracted to. Thinking about it as rationally as I can, I see the point of not contacting someone when you're trying to get your head straight. I stopped messaging Jason as soon as I saw how difficult it was for him once we'd had that brief, exciting, touch. I don't want to compromise him.

I half-smile. Perhaps I'm growing up at last; or maybe I really did – do – care about him. *Am I actually putting him first, before myself?*

I put the dress on. It's dark green, flattering for my colouring; it covers my knees and it has long sleeves. I bought it in Paula's charity shop. It's elegant but sensible; it seems the sort of dress to wear to Rosemary's birthday buffet. Demure, and not at all revealing. *Like a vicar's wife.*

I bumped into Ally earlier today at the market in Fall's End. She's so much more subdued, I could almost like her. She asked if I fancied a coffee, so we went to the King's Arms, the thatched pub on the corner of the road that leads to Smith's Common. We talked a bit about mums and dads. She asked me how I coped, as a teenager, with an unwanted step-parent. I said I didn't really have to, because Mum cleared off with him to Canada. It struck me that I'd not given any recent thought to the sense of unspoken abandonment; saying goodbye to my mum as she went off to a wonderful new life and left me and Dad behind.

'Be happy for me, Meggy!' A dry kiss planted on my cheek. *Happy?*

I've built up some sort of cold, hard shell to stop the pain. It appears that other people, when they try to get close to me, feel the effect of it.

What was it that Jason had once spoken about – toxic cupboards in our lives? If we have something that hasn't been dealt with, it's like a cupboard with poison in it; it tends to leak out and affect the whole house, and whoever we invite into it.

A big thought, and one that I know I need to look into. Perhaps with a spiritual person – not Jason. Maybe I should have a chat with Rev Kathy. I liked her when I met her while we were doing the Passion Play. Honest, open, down to earth . . .

'We should go for a walk sometime,' Ally had said, as we left the pub. Was she really reaching out in friendship?

'Well, we could.' I'd shrugged. 'After all, I don't ride.'

She'd half-smiled. 'We could go to that famous bridge. Jason mentioned it yesterday. He says he's writing an article about it for the parish magazine.'

She saw Jason! Did I feel jealous? Was she trying to wind me up? Suddenly, it just didn't matter. She'd glanced at me; was she trying to gauge my feelings?

'Well, it's your land,' I'd observed. 'Maybe you should ask him for royalties.'

She'd laughed. Not the braying laugh I'd come to know; more genuine somehow.

A new friend; an unexpected connection. Two broken girls with a long way to go.

I look at myself in the mirror again. I suppose Ally will be wearing something short and tight to the party. That's OK. I'm sure she'll look great. I like what I've got on.

Letting go is fine. Releasing your grip on something means there's room for something new.

Whatever that is.

Barny's Story

I have no idea why I want to wear a tie. I suppose it's because my dad gave it to me; blue, it goes with my shirt; or maybe it's because I want to impress someone.

Who? Rosemary? I smile at the idea. Still, she did give me a shove in the right direction when I needed it. Maybe she's not such a bad old trout; after all, she's invited me to her party. Meg will be there. But I'm not trying to impress her, am I? I don't know. It's a waste of time, anyway. No, the tie's fine; I'm honouring my dad.

It was weird, spending so much time with him, noticing how frail he is, and feeling a bit of compassion rather than disgust. That was a first. It seems old age and sickness get you more sympathy than being drunk.

His sister doesn't much like me. Thinks I rejected him, walked away. I did, and I don't like to visit, and when I do, I never stick around. Until now.

I stayed for a few days, kipping on the stained old sofa. Same one as I grew up with. Same carpet. Same everything. Fear has made my dad pack in the drinking but if he starts to feel better, I know he'll be back on the booze. Nothing really changes. Except me, perhaps.

I do feel different. I don't know why. A combination, perhaps, of Nun's Drift and the people there. At my dad's

I was so looking forward to going home – because it *is* home, Nun's Drift; Mrs F's house, the Half Moon, the fields, the woods, that lake near Fall's End . . . Yeah, even the bell-ringing on Wednesdays. Not sure I'll be going to the café anytime soon, though. Still . . . perhaps one day. I'm learning that the only person we can ever really do anything about is ourselves. We just cannot control other people. *You can only make choices for you, Barny.*

I grab my keys and my phone. Then I remember the last conversation I had with Dad's sister, Tasha. I was sitting at the dirty kitchen table, and she sat down opposite, staring at me out of hard, resentful eyes, lighting a cigarette and exhaling.

She'd so casually mentioned my mother.

'You know she passed away, right?'

The shock went through me like a knife.

She'd taken another puff of her cigarette. 'Just as well, eh?'

I'd sat back in my seat, as if I'd taken a body blow.

'Oh, come on, Barny.' She'd looked irritated. 'You know what happened to your dad when she left! She ruined his life! She didn't care about him *or* you. You never wanted to see her, did you?'

I heard Rosemary's words again: *Don't leave it too late.*

Tasha had leaned across the table, her eyes sparkling with anger. She'd started to list all the terrible things my mother did. The men. The affairs.

'Your mother,' she'd said, eventually, in a righteous tone, 'was a waste of space.'

How could *anyone* be a waste of space?

'World's better off without her.' She'd stubbed out her cigarette aggressively in a saucer. 'She was an evil cow.'

She was also my mother.

'She tried to contact us last year,' she'd said, then, with casual callousness. 'Knew she was sick. Wanted to make up. I didn't tell your dad.' A cold smile. 'I took the letter and burnt it.'

What? You had no right to do that! She'd got up from the table, grabbed her coat and looked down her long nose at me.

'Well, *you* weren't here to deal with it, were you? Anyway, don't know why you look so shocked. You hated her, didn't you?'

Did I?

The front door banged as she left.

I thought about having a drink. *No.*

I could hear my dad, calling my name. Almost on autopilot, I went into the sitting room. The telly was on, as ever, too loud, and my dad was sat in his favourite chair, stick at his side.

'Has she said something, Barny? About your mum?' he'd asked, hesitantly, half-rising from his seat.

He still loved Mum. I could see it in his eyes.

'Barny, I'm sorry I never told you she'd passed on. I just . . .'

I'd interrupted him. 'Try to forgive her, Dad. She was only human.'

Did those words really come from me?

He'd sat back in his chair. 'I already did.' Tears fell down his face. I'd felt the urge to hug him – for the first time ever. So I'd held him, still numbed by Tasha's vitriol and recognising the damage unforgiveness had done in me too;

our responses, Dad's and mine, and Tasha's, to something we couldn't control . . . Tasha had spoken about 'waste' but I could see how much wasted energy there'd been in futile and hopeless choices.

'Come and see me again soon, son.'

'Yeah. I will, Dad. OK.'

Now, here I am, wearing his tie and feeling a myriad of emotions. Gratitude, sadness, shock. Jason will be at Rosemary's. He's been a great counsellor. A real friend. Not sure I've ever had many of them. He's introduced me to Rev Mark, a chubby bloke with a good sense of humour. I've started a healing process, I know that; a process of letting go of control, of letting go of the past, and I also know it'll be a long road to recovery. But I won't be travelling it alone.

I look at the half-empty packet of cigarettes on the bed. *Another choice, Barny.* I seize the packet, and chuck it in the bin.

Creaking open the bedroom door with its ancient, old-fashioned latch, I shout down the stairs.

'You ready, Mrs F?'

She appears, smoothing down a floral dress. 'Do I look like mutton dressed as lamb?' she asks. 'Come on, be honest.'

'Nah, you look great. Really.'

'You're just flattering me,' she says, but she looks pleased as she snatches up her flowery umbrella from the stand in the hall.

I open the door for her. 'Come on. We've got a party to go to.'

Rosemary's Story

I'm putting the finishing touches to the table.

'Eleven people at supper! Eleven disciples, weren't there,' says Arthur, humorously, as he plates up the salmon – covered in mayonnaise, very nice – 'minus Judas.' I'm so surprised he's mentioned anything biblical I nearly drop the centrepiece – a large vase full of yellow tulips. I do love tulips, even though it's so depressing when the petals fall off and you're just left with a stalk. Arthur says the muntjacs in the village have devastated the tulips this year. Well, they didn't get mine! They wouldn't dare.

We're entertaining for my birthday. The actual date is tomorrow, when we go on holiday, but tonight's my official party. I've invited Meg, Ally, Jason, Flora, Barny, Daisy, old Alec and Paula. Another guest was a bit last-minute – but Paula's mother agreed to come too. I asked Meg's aunt, as well, but she's had to say no because of family troubles. Archie couldn't make it, either; he's too busy looking after the new black Labrador puppy Jeremy Thompson-Tracey gave him.

'I can't leave the little fella, Floss,' he'd told me, excitement written all over his face and making him look twenty years younger. 'I'm all he's got. And he's tiny. I'm gonna call him Tim. We're gonna have such adventures, you know!'

'I'm sure you are.' I'd watched him grab some puppy mix from the farm shop and dash away.

I thought a buffet was the best idea for tonight, but I don't do the kind of shop-bought pork pie, quiche and crisps event that most people expect. I love the way their eyes dance when they see the great salmon on its dish, and the bowls of salads, all different, not just the usual limp lettuce and cucumber affair.

'Wow, Rosemary!' gasps Meg, arriving first and brandishing a bunch of bright peonies. 'That table's amazing. Look at the size of the salmon!'

I try not to feel proud.

Of course, it took a lot of thinking about; but these are the people I want to be here. My nearest and dearest in the village. Well – to some extent. I told Meg very firmly that I was inviting Barny. She'd seemed a little stunned, but when she'd recovered, she'd nodded. I hope the two of them can be civil. I heard from Flora that Barny's mother unexpectedly passed away so, in the parlance of the young, I'm 'feeling it' for him at the moment.

I've had an interesting conversation with Arthur, too. We were in the pub at Fall's End, our favourite eating place, having a quick chat with Rev Kathy who'd nipped in for a ginger beer before going off for a pastoral visit. I'd congratulated her on the wonderful Passion Play and she'd said she was thinking of doing one next year incorporating Palm Sunday and everything else bar the book of Revelation. I'd smiled as if I was on board with it – I'm not.

Arthur was enjoying his sausage and mash. I don't think sausages are a particularly healthy food choice, but he does so love them!

I had a forkful of sea bass. 'You know, Arthur, vicars work so hard! Jason's single, and so's Kathy – now, don't get any ideas! She's much older than him!' He'd raised an eyebrow. 'Anyway, he's a monk, isn't he, really? But I wonder if Kathy will ever get married again? Someone said she was divorced.' I'd put my fork down and taken a sip of tonic water. 'Must be hard to be married to a vicar. I mean, you get all these needy people knocking on your door . . .'

My husband had laughed. 'And coming to a buffet dinner when your wife's celebrating her birthday.'

'Oh yes. Alright. Well, maybe it's not just vicars . . . still, I mean, it's their job, isn't it? No getting away from it. I wonder Jason hasn't had burnout. He always seems a tad anxious to me. If he hadn't made that promise to be single, I think he and Ally might have . . .'

Arthur was laughing again.

'What?' I'd dug into my sea bass. 'They ride horses together. They obviously get along!' I'd savoured the tomato and chive sauce. Very tasty.

He was shaking his head, drinking his beer.

'What's so funny, Arthur Lane?'

'Can't believe you've missed it.'

'Missed what?'

'Meg and Jason. They *like* each other. But they're not doing anything about it.'

I'd dabbed my mouth and put my napkin down. 'No, Meg liked *Barny*. Jason's just a friend.'

'She fancies the vicar,' my husband had replied, slowly, as if I was a bit simple.

'How on – what? How do you know?'

'I have eyes, Rosey.' They'd twinkled as he'd resumed eating.

So, I have also had to tell Meg that the vicar is coming to the party. She'd swallowed hard but I could tell she didn't want to upset me by not coming. Honestly! What a minefield. How did I miss that attraction between Meg and Jason, anyway? And how come my husband had noticed it? True, he can be very insightful at times, but why didn't I see it? Alright, I knew they were friendly. I even thought he might be good for her, at one stage, much better than Barny Baines. But then of course it came out that he'd taken that vow. When it became common knowledge – how did that happen? I wonder if he's embarrassed that everyone knows? I mean, they do! – I would never have believed he could ever have been *tempted*. I mean, he's a real man of God. I said that to Arthur as we'd left the pub. He'd turned to me with a wry smile, and given me a kiss on the cheek.

'Yes, Rosey, and he's also human.'

'Oh no, I think you're wrong.'

He'd opened the car door, laughing out loud. And as I thought of what I'd said, I'd started to laugh too.

It's pretty awful having to warn people about other guests coming to a party, but I'm determined to have them all there. I popped round to see Paula at the charity shop.

'I suppose you're asking my mother as well?' she'd said, a little defensively.

No! I had a thought. 'Well, as far as I know, you don't come as a package deal. So, I won't, unless you'd like me to.'

That apparent consideration, not in the least motivated by self-interest (oh dear; I don't like the old crow – I must stop calling her that! – and I knew Paula wouldn't want her mother there) had an effect. A slight smile had crossed her saturnine features. *Oh, I do hope she'll be at least a little cheerful at the party!*

'I'll come.' She'd carried on hanging T-shirts on a rail.

I'd coughed. 'Err . . . there's another thing. I've invited Barny.' As if as an excuse, I'd added, 'His mother's died!'

She'd opened her mouth and shut it quickly. I'd wondered if she was going to say *Lucky him!* but she didn't.

'Please still come,' I'd said. 'I know you don't get out m – I mean, I really want you there.'

She'd looked doubtful. Then she'd said, rather reluctantly, 'OK.'

'Well done, Paula! You can't let one man take away your joy,' I'd said, stoutly. 'Anyway – you can chat to Meg and Ally.'

She didn't look too impressed but she'd muttered, 'Well, Meg has been messaging me. She wants to meet for coffee.'

'Wonderful!' I'd exclaimed.

I'd left the shop trying not to think about the grudging, ungrateful acceptance of my invitation. *Rosemary Lane, you weren't going to do any more good to this lot till after your holiday!*

I knew I needed to pray. There was the big church opposite the market square, but I preferred St Saviour's if I needed to talk to the Good Lord in peace; I do so love that stained-glass window of the Good Shepherd! I'd hesitated, remembering that people had been saying just lately that there was a 'nice feeling' at that bridge outside the village, but I was just not prepared to go down there till it hadn't rained for a bit. *I am simply not ruining another pair of boots.*

Anyway, that bridge didn't do much for me. *Maybe you should make a little pilgrimage one day – on your own, no other company.* Not sure where that thought had come from. No! Too many memories at the bridge; I could almost hear the echoing taunts of children: *Flossie, Flossie, silly hair.*

Still, that was then, and this was now. They were just kids. Some of them from struggling families. Jealous of me, perhaps, being an only child with a comfortable home and happy parents. Didn't excuse the teasing, though . . . and at times that could become cruel. But the way I'd reacted wasn't great; isolating myself from the village children, thinking I was better than them, judging them . . .

Later, I got a message from Paula: *Mother wants to come to the party.*

Heart sinking, I felt like messaging back: *Why? So she can keep an eye on you? Or criticise me? Pity you told her about it.* But I'd remembered what I'd said to her, and wrote: *Invite her, if you're happy xx*

No answer.

Another ring of the wonderful doorbell Arthur installed, and I rush to answer it. Flora has arrived with Barny. The words, 'Let battle commence!' come to mind, but I dismiss the thought at once. Barny hands me a bottle of wine, leans forward and surprises me with a quick peck on the cheek.

'Thanks for inviting me,' he says.

He looks thinner, older.

Meg pops her head round the sitting room door and smiles. 'Hey, Barny! Want a drink?'

'Oh, hey.' I've never seen him look so uncomfortable.

I'm not sure what's happened between these two, but it's a tricky moment, so I decide to save the day. I take his arm, and march him past Meg.

'Barny, come on, let me show you the salmon. And I have the most amazing dill and mustard potato salad.'

When everyone's there except for Jason, Meg gets me aside in the hallway.

'Look,' I say, pre-emptively, 'I know he's hurt you, but his mother died!'

She's shaking her head. 'No, you don't understand. It was me. I told him I didn't want him.'

'Oh!' I close the square-paned glass door to the sitting room to ensure some privacy.

'I don't know if I dare say anything to him about his mum.' She reddens a little. 'He doesn't want to talk to me.'

I'm feeling slightly astounded that it's Meg who turned Barny down and not the other way around. *Unbelievable! I got this wrong too!* Honestly, do I know *nothing* about people? I stare at her, biting my glossy lips. *Surely, she doesn't really have strong feelings for the vicar? I mean . . .*

'I thought he wouldn't care too much if I didn't want to date him,' she mumbles. 'But . . .'

'Maybe he liked you more than you thought, then.' When did I start believing someone like Barny could have deep feelings for anyone? *Someone like Barny! Rosemary, listen to yourself!*

She sighs. 'I've got a lot to learn about people, Rosemary.'

I wipe a hand over my face.

'You and me both, Meg!'

All of a sudden, she hugs me. It takes me by surprise but it's not unwelcome.

'You're just magic, you know that?' she says.

'I'm really not,' I say, resignedly, patting her on the back. 'But I'm glad you think so. Come on. Let's try some of Arthur's fruit punch.'

Jason's Story

I love Nun's Drift. I love the people. But I know I have to make changes. I have to have more breaks; more rest; delegate pastoral issues; talk to the team more; visit Father Simon when I can.

I loved the retreat house, too; a beautiful spot in the middle of the Essex countryside. I spent my time walking, and listening, and 'being'. I spoke to Mark a bit, but not a lot. He has his own issues, and it was his time for retreat too.

On the way back, I took a couple of extra days off to go to the priory. Another amazingly tranquil place, an old house, three storeys, its high windows making it look as if it were standing on tiptoes peering over the valley. Only twelve friars live there. The daily rhythm of life was something I enjoyed; as well as walking and talking with Father Simon, a sanguine man in his seventies, about the kind of life I was choosing to live, and how difficult it was to live that life authentically in this world.

It's only now I'm seeing the enormity of the choice I've made. It's like balancing on a precipice; sheer terror. *What have I done?* Seemed so easy when I was younger, in many respects – check out of relationships; concentrate on God. Not always easy, but manageable. Then I met someone.

Of course, it was bound to happen; I just didn't think it through. Meg, and the explosion of thoughts and feelings whenever I'm near her. *We could have had a family.*

Father Simon helps me to put things in perspective. We may not have got along anyway; forbidden fruit always seems so tempting; some people are attracted to the unattainable – what would happen if the unavailable suddenly became available? True. But I didn't expect the powerful feelings. And of course, I failed with the boundaries.

I feel I've let Meg down.

Let myself down.

Let God down.

Father Simon had a brightness in his wise eyes as he started to talk about cars. I really didn't know what he was going on about when he was saying he had the chance to buy an Alfa Sud when he was young, and it looked such a great car, bright yellow, but he couldn't afford the insurance at the time. For years he wished he'd had that car. Then he saw it one day, when he was getting petrol somewhere, with so much rust he couldn't believe it. The dream, the fantasy, really didn't match the reality of what was. The simple allegory spoke to me.

Stop overthinking, Jason! You've really got to be careful with your mind. It can get into all sorts of stories, all sorts of fantasies. Deal with what is. Accept life as it's served, not as you'd like it to be dished up.

I'd made a choice. Perhaps it hadn't been properly thought through regarding the long-term consequences; it could even have been made for wrong reasons.

And yet, maybe not.

Whatever, I was sticking with it.

Now, how to navigate the way forward for my remaining years?

'Look, is there anywhere you can go,' said Father Simon, 'sort of far enough away not to be bothered, but close enough for you to be available if needed? Somewhere you won't be interrupted by too many parishioners walking their dogs?' He'd grinned.

Hmm. Maybe.

This place is beginning to grow on me.

I didn't think much of it when I first encountered it, but now – yes, I see more and more of the beauty; a gradual revealing that sometimes happens in life.

I walk onto the bridge, with its crumbling parapets, and glance down into the still water. It's later in the day, and the ducks are flying in. One, two, three . . . They stir up the water, just like people stir up the stillness of a life, but as I wait, the disturbance subsides as the ducks flip their tails and swim under the bridge. They move on and all is quiet again.

I wander to the other side of the bridge, leaning on the gate, staring into the nothingness beyond. Only it isn't nothingness. It's a big meadow, with wildflowers; so many ox-eye daisies it looks white as far as the eye can see, almost like a snowdrift.

It's not really a bridge to nowhere, is it?

It's just a bridge to something you don't expect.

You think there should be a fine mansion, a priory.

Instead, there's a field.

But the field is beautiful.

Looking back at the rusted metal gates, I think how hard it is, through the burgeoning undergrowth, to find this place, this crossing over into beauty. It's an expansive view one side, limited and overgrown the other; the parapets are crumbling and I'm surprised this bridge isn't labelled as dangerous; it probably is. Should be a warning! Something Jeremy Thompson-Tracey needs to get around to, maybe. At that point, I suspect, the bridge will be shut; no public access.

It's off the beaten path, too; somewhere none of us would normally travel; we'd look for proper footpaths that are easy to traverse. This bridge is a surprise; a vision of yesteryear and yet so relevant today. A bridge crossing from one place to another. *Maybe the life of faith itself is a bit of a bridge; we invite people to find it, and if they want to, we walk with them on it, to something perhaps we, and they, didn't expect.*

I find I'm glad I discovered the bridge at Fall's End.

I'm late to Rosemary's party. When she messaged me who was going, I immediately went into the retreat house chapel and prayed. Inviting Barny seemed to be a very brave decision, given that she'd also asked the Bellwoods – and Meg. But when I get there, expecting to have to do a great deal of peace-making and hoping there wouldn't be shouting, tears and sausage rolls being thrown, there's a rousing cheer. They're pleased to see me!

I'm interested to see that Barny is being well taken care of by Arthur and Alec, men together, closing ranks and protecting someone who is hurt and needs so much help. I can hear them discussing snakes and churchyards, and Alec offering to 'hunt down the viper'. I don't like to mention that I saw this thing and it's just a grass snake. I make a mental note to have a chat with Alec about legally protected, harmless reptiles. But that can wait for another day.

'Have some fruit punch, Vicar!' Rosemary ladles some into a glass and shoves it at me. I take a sip and my eyes water.

'Whoa,' I splutter. 'Fruit? That's strong stuff!'

I realise the fellas are laughing at me; I laugh too.

The remains of an enormous spread are still on the dining table, and Rosemary is fussing over whether there's any of the watercress sauce and quinoa, squash and broccoli salad, and homemade chilli hummus left for me to enjoy. I've never seen so many different types of salad on one table; when she said there was a buffet, knowing Rosemary, I didn't think it would be sausages on sticks, a few pickled onions and nuts, but I didn't expect this. It's a banquet for royalty.

I look at the happy faces all around. No fights, no shouting – thankfully. Even Mrs Bellwood looks comfortable, in a chair next to Flora; she's wearing her hat, and a drab dark dress, and seems half asleep. Rosemary whispers that this is because Paula keeps telling her it's only *fruit* punch and the old lady has consumed rather a lot of it. Paula is actually wearing a smile; one of chilling, knowing satisfaction. I feel momentarily disconcerted.

As I load my plate with good things, I raise my eyes and notice Meg filling her glass. She smiles, and I do too, but that's it. She goes to sit with Paula.

It's over. We both know it. Not that it ever started . . .

Daisy and Ally are giggling together; they stop when they spot me watching, and I wonder what they're laughing about, or who. They both seem embarrassed. I say hello, feeling Arthur's comforting touch on my shoulder as he leaves the room.

Then, someone calls 'hush!' as the lights dim and Arthur brings in the cake. It's huge, someone says it's lemon drizzle, and there's a candle on the top of it. Rosemary, wearing a long, too-tight red dress – she's bursting out of it and I fear for the seams and her modesty – claps her hands in delight. I hear Daisy mutter something about the number of candles that *should* be on it, and fire hazards. Then people are singing *Happy Birthday*.

What a strange mix they are!

So many troubles, all in one room!

And helpers, coming alongside.

I almost feel overwhelmed, so I cram some of the delicious potato and dill salad into my mouth.

'Eat too much of that, you'll get fatter,' Barny observes, helping himself to a large slice of Rosemary's ham and leek pie.

'Eat too much of *that* and you won't have any room for cake,' I reply.

'Oh, I figure you'll be stuffing most of that down your throat anyway,' he says, lightly. 'Won't be anything left for me.'

I glance at him with irony, and wipe my mouth. 'Look, I've got someone I'd really like you to meet.'

It takes a moment for him to answer.

'Mate,' he says slowly, 'I'm really off girls at the minute, yeah?'

'Not a girl. A friar. A monk!'

'Eh? Wait a moment . . .' He runs his hand nervously through his fair hair.

'I'm not suggesting a career change. Just think he might help, you know?' I laugh as I clap him on the shoulder. 'We'll chat later. Alright?'

'There's so much to be done!' complains the hostess.

'I'm sorry, Rosemary,' says Meg, flicking her hair away from her face in the way I find so endearing. I look away, but the conversation continues. 'I can stack the dishwasher . . .'

'No, no, not that. Work to be done – with people! Excuse me . . . Arthur! Leave that, please. Can you go and find Paula's quilted jacket? I think it's on the bed in the spare room. Quick! They're leaving . . .'

'Thank you for a wond'ful eve'nin!' slurs Maureen Bellwood, as Paula pushes her towards the front door. 'I f'give you, you know, Ros'ry. I f'give you – you're wond'ful. Wond'ful!'

'Thank you so much! So glad you could come!' Rosemary shuts the door smartly. 'Oh, thank goodness she's gone. Ah! I am sorry, Vicar, didn't – er – see you there . . .'

'Don't mind me! I've got to go too.'

'Good gracious, that was all more stressful than I thought it would be.' She wipes her brow with her well-manicured hand. 'I wonder if there's any of that punch left.'

I laugh and wish her a very happy birthday. It's only when I get outside that I realise I didn't say goodbye to Meg. I turn back, with just a moment's regret.

'Vicar! Jason!' Arthur appears just as I reach my car. He's out of breath, carrying something. 'You forgot your coat!'

'Thanks!' I take it, and put it on. 'Your wife needs a rest,' I tell him.

'Huh! She needs some boundaries, that's what she needs.'

Boundaries!

'Good advice.' I nod. 'You know, that party went very well – considering.'

'They behaved themselves because they love her,' he remarks, dryly. 'Otherwise – well, who knows.'

Behaving well towards each other because of Someone we love?

I smile as I unlock the car door.

There's a thought.

About the Author

Sheila Jacobs is a writer, editor and award-winning author of more than twenty titles. She writes fiction and non-fiction. She has been involved in the world of Christian publishing for many years as a freelance writer and editor. She enjoys working with new and experienced authors, encouraging them in their writing journey through developmental editing, tips and advice. She is also a speaker, spiritual director and retreat leader (writing and inspirational).

Find out more about Sheila and her work by visiting her website at www.sheila-jacobs.co.uk or on LinkedIn.

Coming soon . . .

The House at Howfield Cross: A Nun's Drift Story.

The group of friends from Nun's Drift, needing space and time to think, decide to go away together to a tranquil place of peace . . . But will they find the answers they're looking for?

The third and final story in the Nun's Drift trilogy.

Also by Sheila Jacobs

Nun's Drift

ISBN 978-1-915046-97-0

A Little Book of Rest

ISBN 978-1-915046-03-1

Watchers

ISBN 978-1-912863-67-9

www.ingramcontent.com/pod-product-compliance
Lightning Source LLC
LaVergne TN
LVHW020047110826
845155LV00029B/658

* 9 7 8 1 9 1 7 4 5 5 5 3 4 *